Only Ever You

Wendy Smith

Photography by Cadwallader Photography

Model Cole Forsgren

Edited by Creative Ink

ISBN-13: 978-1-991303-01-1

Chapter One

Pippa

Age five

I slam my hands onto my hips before raising one hand to wag a finger at the small white animal in the tree.

"Roger. We talked about this. Once you get up there, you can't get back down."

I let out a big sigh as my cat climbs to a higher branch and gives a long, loud *meow*.

Rolling my eyes, I step onto the base of the tree and look closer. "Roger?"

He's pacing. *Stupid cat.*

I wrap my hands around the lowest limb I can reach and pull myself up.

The next branch is harder, but there are some good places to put my feet on the tree, so I scrabble up. Roger's still higher than me.

He lets out a wail. He's stuck.

If I could just climb a little bit higher ...

"Whatcha doing, Pipsqueak?"

I freeze before slowly turning around.

My brother, Lucas, stands at the foot of the tree, his arms crossed.

But it's not him speaking. His best friend, Deacon, waits beside him, one eyebrow raised.

"Roger's up the tree."

Lucas snorts. "Why did you ever call your cat Roger?"

"Because I can." I cross my arms and frown at him.

"It's a stupid name."

The branch jolts, and I let out a scream before dropping my arms to my sides and gripping the wood.

Lucas laughs, but Deacon takes a step forward.

"You okay up there, Pipsqueak?" he asks.

"No." I sniff.

Deacon holds up his arms. "Drop down. I'll catch you."

I shake my head. "I can't. I'm scared."

"Trust me."

Lucas moves beside him, reaching out his arms too. "Come on, Pippa. We've got you."

Big, fat tears roll down my cheeks. "I just wanted to save Roger."

"I'm pretty sure Roger is fine." Deacon beckons me with his fingers. "Jump."

I close my eyes and push myself off the branch. I'm not sure I trust either of them to catch me, but maybe they can ...

Oof.

I land on something soft and slowly open my eyes.

Somehow, they've caught me between them, and we've fallen in a heap on the ground.

I let out a delighted laugh and even grumpy Lucas smiles.

"I'm sorry," I whisper.

Lucas wraps his arms around me. "As long as you're safe, little sis."

He plants a kiss on my cheek, and I giggle. "Thank you for saving me."

"That's what big brothers are for."

A loud crack above us makes both Lucas and me look up. Deacon's scaled the tree, reaching the branch Roger's on, and he's got one arm out to grab him.

Roger loves Deacon, and before I know it, he's rubbing himself on Deacon's hand. Deacon grabs him and drops down off the tree in an instant.

I hold my arms out for Roger, and he comes to me, purring so loudly and headbutting my face.

"Don't climb the tree again, Pipsqueak. You'll hurt yourself. Let one of us do it," Deacon says.

Lucas rolls his eyes. "Don't make her promises like that."

"Why not? You don't want your sister hurt, do you?"

He shuffles on his feet. "No."

I love Deacon.

Chapter Two

Deacon

Age twelve

"Have you seen Katie Peters?" Lucas asks.

I shake my head. We've spent summer hanging out together before our move across the other side of town last week. I'm not sure what I'm going to do without my best friend being right next door.

"She got boobs over the summer. Sprouted out of nowhere. I'm so asking her out."

I snort. "As if you're allowed to date yet."

"Boobs?"

Lucas glares at his little sister. She's so quiet, sitting on the deck beside the table we're lounging around. She's holding a crayon in her hand, her hazel eyes flicking between me and Lucas.

"Go back to your colouring, Pippa. This is grown-up conversation," Lucas growls.

Anyone else might feel threatened by his tone, but Pippa bursts out laughing and shakes her head, her dark pigtails flapping around. "Stop being silly, Lucas. You're a kid."

He goes to stand, and I shove him back in his seat. "What the hell are you doing?"

"She's making fun of me." He puffs out his chest. "*Some* people think I'm very grown up."

I roll my eyes. "She's five. Leave her alone." Shifting my gaze to Pippa, I nod toward the picture she's colouring. "That's a cool cat. Is that Roger?"

She shakes her head. "No, silly. Roger's white. This cat's black."

I chuckle.

"Why are you being so nice to her?" Lucas asks.

I turn toward him. "Because you're lucky you have a little sister. I don't have anyone."

His face falls. "You have me."

"I have both of you." I tilt my head. "You're like family."

A tearing sound behind us makes us both turn, and Pippa stands, a piece of paper in her hand. "This is for you, Lucas."

She hands him a picture of a black kitten. It's a good effort from her—mostly inside the lines, and she beams at him as if she's just painted the Mona Lisa.

"For me?" His whole attitude changes, and he smiles.

"I was going to give it to Deacon, but you're the grumpy one today." She grabs hold of his arm and hugs it. "I love you."

Lucas, who'd just been scowling at her, lights up like a Christmas tree. "I love you too, Pippa."

She pokes my arm with an index finger. "The next picture is for you."

I give her a gentle smile. "I'd like that very much."

"I'm going to draw a dragon for you."

My brow dips as I tilt my head. "A dragon?"

"You and Lucas would fight a dragon if we saw one."

I laugh. "Pipsqueak, when would we see a dragon?"

Her hazel eyes widen and she holds up her palms, her fingers splayed. "They could be anywhere."

Lucas shakes his head. "Mum's reading her a book about dragons at the moment."

"Dragons?" I say, stroking my chin. "I think there's a dragon behind you."

Pippa lets out a squeal, and Lucas glares at me with a 'What the fuck' expression, but I laugh, leaping out of my chair and tickling Pippa.

"That's not fair." She screams with laughter.

I let go, and Lucas shoots her an affectionate look.

"We'll slay the dragons, Pip," Lucas says.

She places her hand on her heart. "Whew."

"Deacon." Lucas's dad walks toward us. "I'm just heading out to grab some fish and chips. Want me to drop you home for dinner?"

"That'd be great, Mr Chapman."

"Daddy, can I come?" Pippa looks at me before switching her gaze to her father.

He reaches down and bops her on the nose. "Not today, Pipsqueak. Your mother wants you inside."

She pouts.

"Come on, Pip. Let's go and see what Mum wants." Lucas stands and holds out his fist for me to bump. "Catch you later, Deac."

The car ride is quiet. I say nothing, and Mr Chapman shoots a glance at me every so often.

Life at home isn't good right now.

"Will you be okay?" he asks as we pull into the driveway.

The Chapmans aren't stupid. They know my parents fight.

I nod. "I'll be fine. Thanks for the ride."

"Any time, son."

I scramble out of the car and take a deep breath before I pull open the screen door. Mr Chapman backs down the driveway, but he's not even at the mailbox before I hear my mother screech.

"Would it kill you to pay attention to me?"

Dad sighs. "I do, Elise. It's just never enough."

Bypassing the living room where they're arguing, I race upstairs to my room.

I close the door, sliding down to the floor behind it, my hands over my ears.

Sometimes I wish I could go and live with Lucas. His parents sometimes argue, but it never gets as bad as my mum and dad.

I'm not even sure why they're together, but my dad says he loves my mum more than anything and that some people just argue.

Whatever it is, I hate it.

Chapter Three

Pippa

Aged twelve

"I don't care what plans you had. You have to take care of your sister today. Your mother and I are away for the weekend. You agreed to this at the start of summer, Lucas."

Curling myself up in a ball as Dad's voice carries through the house, I wish I was anywhere else but here.

Lucas has a giant chip on his shoulder right now. He never used to. We all used to be a big, happy family, but the past couple of years, there's been nothing but tension between him and my parents.

Dad's right. At the start of summer, he and Mum told us they were going away for their wedding anniversary, and Lucas promised he'd be here because I'm not old enough to be left home alone.

The pay-off is that he gets an upgrade to the crappy car he got for his sixteenth birthday—he'll be going to university after the holidays, and that heap of junk might be fine for around town but not so much long-distance.

"I didn't know it was this weekend. I have plans."

"Cancel them."

I don't have to see him to know Lucas is rolling his eyes. He's so ungrateful, and where we used to be close, this growing resentment he has toward me really hurts. I love my big brother, and it's not my fault there's a seven-year age gap between us.

Last week, he made me cry by telling me I was an accident. Mum and Dad reassured me that wasn't true, and I don't really care if it was, but the way he said it was so nasty and cruel, I wondered if my brother had been possessed.

No doubt his plans for the weekend include going to Deacon's place. Those two hang out playing console games and drinking beer, which I know Dad doesn't approve of, but Deacon's mother is pretty lax when it comes to that, so Lucas makes the most of it.

I'd be happy to stay home alone—all I'm going to do is read, but they're insistent he babysit me.

At the thought of that, I roll my eyes. I think I'm more mature than he is most times.

"Fine!" Lucas yells. "Hurry up, Pippa."

I put my book on my lap. "Hurry up? Where are we going?"

"The Millers. Get your arse in the car."

"Lucas. That's no way to talk to your sister," Dad yells.

I let out a sigh. "Okay. Whatever. I'm coming."

After grabbing my backpack off the floor, I drop the book I'm reading into it. I choose another couple of books, because God only knows how long a visit to the Millers will take, and place them into the bag before slinging it over my shoulder.

I stalk out to his car and drop my bag on the floor as I slide into the passenger seat.

He slams the driver's door, and without saying a word, pushes the key into the ignition and starts the car.

"You know, once they're gone you can just bring me home."

He snorts. "Dad'll kick my arse if I do that."

"They don't need to know."

As he pulls out of the driveway, he lets out a loud sigh. "Pippa, you're my responsibility whether I like it or not. It'll just be for a few hours, and you can stay in the car if you want."

I screw up my face. "The hot car that smells of boy germs?"

"You can't come inside with us. This is going to be the most boring afternoon of your life."

"Just as well I brought books with me then."

He glares at me. "If you come inside, I'll tell Deacon you've got a massive crush on him."

My cheeks burn hot. "Why are you so mean?"

"I see you doodling hearts on your books. It's so pathetic. You're twelve. He'll never be interested in you."

I cross my arms. "You're such a dick."

The rest of the ride is silent. Lucas ignores me right up until we pull into the driveway.

I'm more than a little in love with the Miller house. Unlike our single-level, three-bedroom humble home, theirs is a white two-storey house with verandahs running around both levels. It reminds me of a wedding cake.

Mrs Miller's passionate about her garden, and with the white picket fence along the front of the yard, it's my fairytale house.

I don't come here very often—Deacon's usually at our place. It's not like my nineteen-year-old brother and his best friend invite me to hang out with them.

Sliding out of the passenger seat, I grab my bag and stalk Lucas to the door. I'd much rather be at home, curled up on the couch reading, but my parents won't let me stay home alone for at least another two years.

Deacon's mum opens the door. She flicks a glance at me, her lips clamped in a straight line. "Your sister's with you?"

He shrugs. "Mum and Dad have gone away to bond or some shit. I promised to look after her. Didn't think I could just leave her at home."

She nods. "I understand." Turning to me, she smiles. "Pippa, how about I grab you a cool drink and a snack?"

I give her at tight smile. "That would be great, thank you. I'm just planning on reading."

Her smile widens. "The swing seat is perfect for that. I'm often out here with my nose in a good book."

"Thanks, Mrs Miller."

Lucas shoots me a glare. "Stay here. We don't need you getting in our way."

I roll my eyes.

"Just be the lookout, Pip. Call out if anyone shows up."

Exasperated, I huff out a breath, running my hand down my face. "Whatever."

He disappears inside the house. Mrs Miller smiles at me again before she closes the screen door.

Stupid boys and their stupid games.

At least soon Lucas will be off to university. The only downside is that means Deacon will be too. I know he'll never look at me as anything other than Lucas's little sister, but he's never impatient or unkind to me.

I let out a sigh.

He's perfect.

He's also nineteen and not about to fall in love with a twelve-year-old. I know that.

While other girls my age might flirt with older boys, I'm not that dumb.

Mrs Miller reappears with a tall glass of juice and a plate with some biscuits on it. "Here we go, Pippa. If you ask me, it's much nicer out here instead of being cooped up in the house." She places them on a small round table not far from the swing seat.

Pulling the table closer, she motions to the seat. "This is the perfect spot in the shade with a lovely breeze coming through. Call out if you need anything else."

"I think I'll be fine. Thank you."

Her smile widens. "You're welcome."

And then I'm left in the quiet of the summer day. Mrs Miller was right about one thing—I'd much rather be out here in the shade than inside on a day like today.

Taking a sip of the juice, I lean back in the seat and inhale a deep breath before grabbing my bag and pulling out my book.

I'm likely to be alone for hours, so I stretch out and get to reading.

It's warm out there—the heat of the sun can still be felt in the shade of the verandah. But there's a cool breeze and before long, I'm closing my book and my eyes.

I wrinkle my nose when something brushes against it.

As I force my eyelids open, Deacon comes into focus, a grin on his lips and his index finger an inch from my face.

"Hey, Pipsqueak. What are you doing here?"

Bouncing my gaze between the door leading into the house and Deacon, I shoot him a quizzical look. "I thought ..."

"We reached our fishing spot when Dad got a call from work. He's just grabbing his things and heading out. Why are you here? Lucas driving you crazy?"

I shake my head. "No, I—"

A roar from inside the house catches our attention, and seconds later, Lucas comes flying out the front door. His boxer shorts and bare chest are confusing. Seconds later, his jeans and shirt soar through the air from above.

What the hell?

Lucas picks up his clothing and drags on his jeans, his eyes fixed on me the whole time. "Some lookout you turned out to be."

Deacon's head spins my way, and if looks could kill, I'd be six feet under. The pain and anguish in his expression—his eyes full of hurt and anger—are enough to make my stomach ache.

Me?

He thinks I had something to do with whatever this is.

I shake my head. "Deacon, I—"

"Whatever." He storms into the house, the doorjamb rattling as he slams the door behind him.

Pressing my hands over my ears, I try my best to shut out the yelling coming from inside as hot tears spill down my cheeks.

I'm not even sure what happened—everything's a blur.

"Get in the car." Lucas stalks off, and I shove my book back in my bag, stumbling as I trip over my own feet in an attempt to get to him before he drives off and leaves me.

He already has the car started, and I run to the passenger side before tugging open the door and throwing myself inside.

The tyres squeal as he takes off, and I scramble to buckle my seatbelt before my idiot brother kills us both.

"This is *your* fault," Lucas grumbles. "If you'd just said something when they pulled in."

"I don't even know what's going on," I sob.

"Elise loves *me*." He slams his fist on the dashboard. "Not that piece of shit she's married to."

My eyes widen. "What ... what are you talking about?"

"Everything was fine until *he* caught us."

I blink rapidly. Nothing makes sense. I'm twelve. I know about sex. I knew my brother was having sex—he's nineteen. But with Deacon's mother?

Nausea sweeps my body. "You ... you were sleeping with Mrs Miller?"

He flicks his angry gaze at me before staring at the road again. "We love each other."

"That's gross."

The brakes squeal, and the seatbelt cuts into me as I'm flung forward. Lucas's Toyota Corolla might be old, but he babies it, and I've never heard the brakes make that noise.

"Get out of my car." He grits his teeth.

"But we're—"

"Out!" he yells.

"Lucas, Mum and Dad are gonna—"

"They're already going to kill me after *you* let us get caught."

"This isn't my fault," I wail.

"Don't be such a baby, Pippa. You could have stopped all this, but no. I bet you had your nose buried in one of those damn books."

The tyres squeal this time as he takes off, and I hold my sobs in, trembling as I grip the seatbelt. Is he taking us home? Ever since Lucas started driving, he's been careful with me in the car. But now he just doesn't care as he flings it around corners until we finally reach the safety of home.

As soon as he comes to a stop, I throw the door open before unbuckling my belt and grabbing my bag. Running to the front door, I fumble in my bag for the house key, and before Lucas can follow, I run to the back of the house—to the safety of my room.

I throw myself on my bed and let my tears flow, gnawing my fisted hand to stop myself making too much noise.

The door swings open with a *snick*, and a loud meow tells me Roger's here. He always announces his arrival as if he needs to tell the world.

And he's exactly what I need right now.

I get up and close the door—properly this time, while Roger jumps on the bed.

When I join him, he rubs around me, purring loudly. I'm sure he just wants food, but for now I'll take his affection.

It doesn't take long before I'm all cried out and exhaustion takes over.

Sleep claws at me before it finally pulls me under.

———

The scent of bacon wafts through the air, and I open my eyes and take a deep breath before memories of yesterday come flooding back.

Why, Lucas? Why would you do that?

Deacon's haunted expression brings tears to my eyes.

My stomach rumbles, and I roll out of bed still dressed in yesterday's clothes and not caring.

Lucas sits at the table, scooping food into his mouth at the rate of knots. He casts a wary gaze over me.

"If you're looking for the bacon, I've already eaten it all."

I glare at him. "You're such a dick."

"You fucked up yesterday."

With a roll of my eyes, I head to the fridge. He really has taken all the remaining bacon, and my stomach growls again as if to punish me.

Settling for cereal, I pour some cornflakes into a bowl and with my gaze fixed on him, I drain the remaining milk. As I set the bowl on the table, it slops over the edge and Lucas snorts.

"You're such a child."

"Look who's talking."

"Mum and Dad are coming back early."

I raise an eyebrow. "I didn't tell."

He shakes his head. "I know you didn't. Mr Miller must have called them."

"Oh, shit."

Lucas laughs. "I think that's the first time I've ever heard you swear, Pip."

Scowling, I scoop up cereal onto my spoon and take a couple of mouthfuls before answering. "I think this is the right time for swearing. Mum and Dad's weekend was to give them a break, and now look at what they're coming back to."

He drops his gaze. For the first time guilt crosses his expression, and he studies the kitchen tabletop before rising and heading down the hallway toward his bedroom.

Half an hour later, the back door opens, and my stomach sinks at the sight of my father. This is the last thing we all need—Dad upset.

"Lucas. Where are you?" he calls.

"Dad?"

He gives me a sad smile. "Hi, sweetheart. Are you okay?"

I nod.

He walks toward me and reaches down, brushing the back of his knuckles against my cheek. "I'm sorry you got caught up in all of this."

"Mr Miller called you?"

He lets out a sigh. "He did. Your mum's on her way inside too. I need to know where your brother is."

I shrug. "Around here somewhere, I think. His car's still there."

"Lucas," he yells before turning back to me. "Maybe you should go to your room for a while. This isn't going to be nice."

I swallow hard and nod again before heading toward my room.

Closing my eyes, I hold my hands over my ears when the yelling starts. A door slams, and footsteps fall outside my door before it opens.

"Oh, Pippa. I'm so sorry, love."

Mum wraps her arms around me, and I bury my face in her neck.

"What's happening?"

She blows out a long breath. "Dad's angry. Lucas is angry. It'll settle down, but I know how you feel about Deacon."

Hot tears spill over my cheeks. "He's my friend too."

"Yes, but I know you've had a crush on him for a very long time. There's so much wrong with what Lucas did, but he also didn't think about you getting hurt in all of this. And that makes me mad."

I raise my head and swipe the tears away. "He blamed me. I didn't know what was going on."

She places a kiss on my forehead. "I know. He's got himself into a bit of a mess."

"What's going to happen?" I ask.

Her eyes grow sad. "The Millers' marriage is over. That's all I know so far. Deacon will be going to university as planned, but what his father will do, I'm not sure yet."

We sit in silence for a moment.

"Mum?"

She strokes my hair. "Yes, sweetie?"

"Are you and Dad okay?"

"Your dad and I are fine. Neither of us are going anywhere."

———

Deacon's father is leaving today.

It's been a week since he caught Lucas with Mrs Miller, and while my parents say they're not keeping anything from me, I'm up-to-date with what's going on through eavesdropping on whispered conversations.

I need to see Deacon.

It takes me half the day, but I walk across town to Deacon's house. He *has* to know that I knew nothing about it.

I have to make things right.

Deacon's car sits in the driveway, the boot up. As I pass, I glance at the boxes inside. He stalks from the house to the car, not looking my way at all.

"Deacon?"

He turns, glowering at me, and I take a step back.

"Are you okay?" I ask.

"Nope. No thanks to you and your brother."

"But I didn't—"

"Don't bother coming over here again, Pippa. Dad and I are leaving for good." He turns back to the boot of the car and starts moving around boxes.

Tears prick my eyes. "Where are you going?"

He lets out a frustrated sigh. "Hamilton. Dad's got a friend who can get him into the power plant there, and it'll be closer to Auckland for uni."

I blink, unable to speak. He's leaving and he's angry with me.

This is such a mess, and I'm not to blame for any of it.

When I sniff, he turns around again and his brows knit as I wipe my nose with the back of my sleeve.

"Hell, I'm sorry, Pippa. But the damage Lucas has done ... it's irreversible. And I can't ignore the part you played in it even though I'm sure you thought you were just being loyal to your brother."

Tears roll down my cheeks, and he grips my arms.

"I know you'll miss me, Pipsqueak. I'll miss you too." After planting a kiss on the top of my head, he lets go of me and reaches for the boot lid before closing the back of the car.

"Dad. I'm ready," he calls.

His father appears at the back door, gives me a mournful look, and nods. "I'm right behind you, son."

Deacon climbs into his car, and his father ruffles my hair as he walks past. "Give my regards to your parents, Pippa. Take care."

The cars start up, and Deacon drives away without a backward glance, followed by his father.

I trudge down the driveway and out onto the footpath.

My head's still spinning with everything that went down.

Mum and Dad are so angry with Lucas. I'm not speaking to him. I can't. While I knew Deacon would be away for university, he's taken him away from me forever.

Heartbroken, I look back at the house where it all fell apart.

Mrs Miller's standing at the window, peering out of it as her husband and son drive away.

I hate her.

Starting the long walk home, tears fall down my cheeks.

I swipe them away with my palms, but they keep coming.

When a familiar car pulls up beside me, I come to a stop, slamming my arms across my chest.

My brother opens the driver's door and climbs out, staring at me from across the roof. "Get in. Mum's on the warpath and you disappearing hasn't helped her mood at all."

Still sulking, I open the passenger door and slide into the seat. After buckling my seatbelt, I cross my arms again and look out the window.

"I know where you've been," Lucas says.

I say nothing. There's no point. He's hurt me with his actions as well as Deacon and his father.

"Damn it, Pippa. Talk to me."

Tears well in my eyes again, but I have nothing to say to Lucas.

"I know you love Deacon. He's been my best friend since you were little. But he's made his choice, and I made mine. I'm sorry you got stuck in the middle."

I clamp my lips together. No. He doesn't get my words. I'm not even going to acknowledge him. It's not just Deacon and his father whose hearts are broken.

The rest of the ride home is silent.

I might not ever speak with Lucas again.

Chapter Four

Deacon

Twelve years later

Another day, another invitation.

This time, it's my old high school having a reunion. As if I'd ever set foot in Gisborne ever again.

She lives there.

While she might be my biological mother, she's also the woman who broke my dad. He was never the same after we left. He worked himself into the ground at the power plant until he died six years ago.

I'm just glad he saw the fruits of my labour—mine and a group of uni friends who made an alcohol-free beer that went viral and became a multi-million-dollar company.

"Simone," I call out.

Simone, my PA, appears in the doorway. She places her hands on her hips and gives me a bored look as if she knows exactly what I'm about to say.

I hold up the invitation. "Could you please write them back *again* and tell them I'm not interested in this stupid reunion?"

She shakes her head.

We've been working together for two years, and why she's still here, I'll never know. I can be a perfectionist, and I've got no patience for things that waste my time—like this. She's got her eyes on the big prize—becoming the CEO's PA instead of the lowly CTO. But Garrett's already started advertising for an external candidate, and I'm far too selfish to suggest the woman I'm dependent on to him.

"Why don't you write to them? They're clearly not taking the polite brush-off very well."

I snort. "I'm not sure why they're so focused on me giving any kind of speech. I sucked at that kind of thing when I was at school."

A smile sweeps her lips, before she laughs. "You're so eloquent. I have no idea why they'd want you either."

"It's a mystery." I drop the letter to the desk and hold up my palms.

Simone rolls her eyes and stalks across the room. "Give it to me. I'll write a reply in Deacon speak."

"Deacon speak?" I side-eye her, and she laughs again.

"The only question really is how many ways I can find to say, 'Fuck off'?"

I chuckle. "You know me so well."

With another eye-roll, she picks up the piece of paper and turns to leave. "Just remember your board meeting starts in about ten minutes."

Saluting her, I rise from my seat. "I suppose I should go and get a coffee before I head in there."

"Good luck."

Ten minutes later, I join Garrett and Victor in the boardroom. The only one missing now is Mallory—Garrett's ex and marketing manager extraordinaire.

Victor eyes my coffee. "I knew I should have made a stop before the meeting."

I take a sip of my drink. "You snooze, you lose."

He scowls as I take my seat.

"Hey Garrett, have you found a new PA yet?"

Garrett fixes his gaze on me. "Why? Are you ready to give up yours?"

I snort. "Not likely."

"Actually, there's a candidate coming in tomorrow. The recruitment company's done a good job of weeding out the nopes this time. This one's perfect on paper at least, so I'm hoping it'll be a quick process."

"Thank God for that," Victor says. "Do you remember that dipshit they tried sending us for the accounting role?"

I laugh. Vic had nothing but trouble the last time he looked for a new assistant accountant. One guy in particular managed to bluff his way through the entire recruitment process until he interviewed with Vic.

Then it became painfully obvious that he thought he could just wing it.

Needless to say, Vic came down hard on the company we were using.

"Anyway, my candidate tomorrow is perfect. She's from Gisborne too. I brought her file down on the off chance that you know her and can shorten this whole process."

I roll my eyes. "You know as well as I do that's not likely. I haven't been back there since I was nineteen."

He pushes the file across the table. A hazel-eyed gaze stares at me from the photo attached to the front.

Wait a minute.

I know those eyes.

I frown, opening the folder.

Philippa Theresa Chapman.

"No way." I meet Garrett's gaze.

His brows knit before he bursts out laughing. "You do know her."

That photo. She's gorgeous. That was inevitable for Pippa. She was a pretty girl, so full of life and love and everything good in the world. Her dark hair is swept up into a bun with loose wisps of it falling down the sides of her face. That smile of hers could light the darkest of places.

Lucas would hate it if I hurt her.

It would be the ultimate payback.

That thought, however brief, sits on my chest and aches. No. I couldn't do that to her. She doesn't deserve it.

I close the folder and lean back in my chair. "How do you feel about taking Simone taking the role?"

Vic smirks.

The boardroom door swings open and Mallory walks in. The only woman in our group—she was dating Garrett when we came up with our revolutionary business idea and given she was studying marketing at the time, it was a no-brainer for her to join us.

She's often the one who grounds us—pointing out when we're getting out of control. She might not be with Garrett anymore, but we're all good friends.

"Can we get this meeting going? I've got an appointment with a new billboard company this afternoon."

"We've been waiting on you." Garrett rolls his head on the head-rest of his chair.

"Deacon was just about to tell us why the woman interviewing tomorrow for Garrett's PA role is a bad choice," Vic says.

Mallory huffs out a breath. "Let me guess. You've had sex with her?"

"That's not a barrier to employment." I grin. "She's my ex-best friend's sister."

A collective *oooh* goes around the table. These are my people. They know my story.

"The ex-best friend who fucked your mum?" Garrett asks.

I nod slowly. "The very same."

"So, you want me to get HR to drop the interview? Is that why you're offering me Simone, who I might add would also be perfect for the role?" He beams as if the idea hasn't occurred to him before.

"No. I want Pippa as my PA."

Every eye in the room swivels to me.

I shrug. "What? She was twelve when it happened. It wasn't her fault. I was angry at her back then, but she didn't do anything except love her brother."

"You didn't even look at her CV," Garrett says.

"I'll take it back to my office with me. But she was a smart kid. Always had her nose in a book."

Mallory rolls her eyes. "Lord help us."

I lean forward, stitching my fingers together. "Now. Let's get this meeting underway."

Chapter Five

Pippa

"The situation's changed."

My stomach drops.

I went through the whole initial interview process not knowing who the company was that I was applying for. That was kept secret.

When I found it was Infinity Drinks, I had a sinking feeling I wouldn't get the job.

Of course I knew all about the company Deacon co-founded. He might have been half an island away, but I followed his career. It made me proud to see how well he'd done for himself. He deserved everything good after the mess his mother made of his life.

The last time I saw Deacon Miller, he still thought I was in on that mess. It wasn't until I was older that I realised assigning blame to a twelve-year-old was messed up, but he wasn't really that much older.

I almost pulled my job application, never expecting they'd ask me in for an interview.

Now I'm here with the head of Infinity HR, Rochelle, who tells me as soon as I've sat down that the situation's changed.

It's not rocket science to assume that Deacon's involved.

"I understand."

She smiles, and I'm about to open my mouth to thank her for the opportunity when she drops a bombshell.

"As you know, the PA role was for the CEO, but due to an internal promotion, it's now PA for the CTO."

What?

I pored over the corporate website so many times looking for any new information on Deacon. He's the CTO.

"I'm sorry?"

She nods. "Don't panic. The salary and benefits are all the same. It's just an internal thing, but I thought it was important that you know."

"Thank you?"

"Let's get on with this interview and Mr Miller has asked that we go up to his office afterward."

My heart thuds.

I knew if I got the job I'd see Deacon at some point, but that doesn't mean I'm prepared to do it today.

"Okay, then, Philippa. I see from your application you have a Bachelor's in business. Have you ever considered applying for our intern program? It's something you could do in future if you're interested."

"I ... uh ... Please call me Pippa."

She smiles. "Okay, Pippa. Same question."

I'm not sure how I make it through the next hour, but Rochelle seems happy with my answers. Yes, I might consider applying as an intern at some point. Yes, I'm perfectly happy applying for a PA role despite my qualifications—I've done it before, and I want to get some work experience under my belt. And so on.

After all the questions are answered and we make small talk for a few minutes, she leads me to the elevator and presses up.

Butterflies take over my stomach and I blow out a long breath.

"Nervous?" Rochelle asks.

I nod, unable to speak.

"You'll be fine. The executive management are great." She smiles. "They're a group of uni friends who have worked together to build the company. It's all fantastic product, and the perks of working here are amazing."

"Sounds perfect." I manage to get the words out, but inside my heart is racing.

The elevator dings, and the doors open.

Here we go.

I scrape the palms of my hands with my nails. I didn't think I'd come into contact with Deacon so soon. I'm so not ready.

We walk down a corridor before she opens a door and I follow her into an outer office. A desk sits by the door I assume leads to Deacon's office.

I draw in a deep breath before she knocks briefly and then pushes it open.

She's in my way, so I can't see Deacon yet. Anticipation makes me quite faint. It's been so long since I've seen him in the flesh and he's not just a picture on a website.

"We've just finished our interview. You wanted to see Pippa?"

"Yes."

Rochelle steps out of the way and ushers me through.

Deacon rises from behind his desk.

Oh my.

The years have been good to him. He was always a good-looking boy, but as a man he's devastatingly handsome.

His dark hair is short at the sides, a little longer on top. Last time I saw him, he was clean-shaven, but his short-trimmed beard makes him look so grown up. Although, I guess he's now in his early thirties.

He smiles widely, and it reaches his sparkling blue eyes.

"Pippa." His warm tone washes over me, and my heart calms a little. I always wondered what it would be like to see him again. Would he still be angry? Would he blame me?

"Deacon. It's good to see you." It's hard to smile. Why is it so hard to smile?

Maybe because this whole thing is awkward.

"Hey, Rochelle. Mind giving me a minute with Pippa?"

Her gaze flicks between us, and she nods. "Sure. I'll just wait outside and walk you back down when you're finished."

I meet her eyes and give her what I hope is a reassuring smile. "Thank you."

Her brows knit as she turns before she closes the door.

Deacon rounds the desk until he's standing in front of me. I can't meet his gaze. I'll melt into a puddle on the floor if I do.

"Hey, Pipsqueak."

My lips part, but nothing comes out.

He raises his hand and tucks a lock of hair that's escaped behind my ear.

His smile's so open and welcoming. A far cry from the last time I saw him.

"Miss me?"

"I thought I could handle this," I whisper, biting my inside cheek to stop myself welling up.

"It's good to see you," he says. "Are you going to come and work with me?"

I shrug. "I didn't think you'd want me to."

"Are you kidding?" He grasps my chin and pulls my gaze to meet his. "I can trust you to keep me in line, can't I?"

I blink rapidly, my smile still hiding from him.

"Seriously, Pip. I read your CV. You're perfect for the job and I get to see my girl every day. What could be better?"

He pops a kiss on my nose and lets go of my chin.

His affectionate action releases the tension, and I grin. "You're weird."

"That's nothing new." He laughs—*laughs*, and I'm really not sure what to make of him after all this time.

"The last time I saw you, you were angry with me."

Deacon cocks his head. "I was angry with the world. My family had just been torn apart. But it's been twelve years, and I'm glad to see you. Even happier if I can make you get me coffee."

I roll my eyes, and he laughs again.

"There's my girl. Start tomorrow?"

"We haven't talked about a start date."

He grabs my hand. "Well, I am. Come in a little later, maybe ten o'clock, and we'll go for morning tea. You can catch me up on your life."

"So ... I've got the job?"

His smile gives me butterflies. "There's no one else I'd want."

He walks me to the door, opens it, and waves me through. "See you tomorrow morning, Pippa. Around ten."

Rochelle's eyebrows rise as I approach her. "I assume that means you made a hiring decision," she says to him.

"It's a no-brainer. Pippa and I go way back."

It's clear no one's told her this as understanding crosses her features. "You do?"

"He knew me when I was a kid," I say. "We haven't seen one another in years."

She crosses her arms and raises her eyebrows at him. "Explains a lot."

"Bye, Pippa. See you tomorrow."

With a laugh, she walks me to the elevator. "Let's go down to my office and we'll finalise the paperwork."

The butterflies have lessened, but a few still linger.

I'm not sure I can work with this version of Deacon. He's not as moody as I thought he'd be. In fact, he's about the opposite.

If I didn't know better, I'd think he was being flirty.

Chapter Six

Deacon

Philippa Theresa Chapman has knocked my socks off.

Her photo was pretty enough, but when she walked in the door with Rochelle, I was mesmerised.

Pippa was always going to be a beauty. I watched her grow up and knew her brother and I would end up taking an active interest in who she dated.

But now she's a woman—curvy as sin with an hourglass figure and cleavage I'd love to drown in. Her features were always dainty, but her full lips are just begging to be kissed.

Lucas would hate it if I seduced his sister, but any thoughts of revenge for his actions are fleeting as I could never do that to Pippa. She's worth far more than a quick roll in the hay.

As soon as I saw her, there was no way I could stay away. I had to be near her.

She's going to be mine.

Leaving her was hard the first time. She was way too young for me, and I didn't harbour romantic thoughts about her, but I'd known her for her whole life. Pippa was like a sister to me, but I'm not feeling anything sisterly about her now.

When we've made plans to meet for morning tea the next day, I open my office door. Rochelle stands awkwardly in the outer office, meeting my gaze and arching an eyebrow at me while Pippa explains what we are to one another.

My eyes drop to Pippa's hips as she walks away. The sway of them is hypnotising—I foresee a lot of watching those curves in the future.

Should I have interfered with Garrett's hiring process?

No.

Should I have offered up my PA so I could keep Pippa close to me?

Also no.

But I did, and I have no regrets.

An hour later, Rochelle knocks on my office door and walks in. Any smile she had on her face earlier is gone. "I want to ask you what your intentions are toward Pippa, but that makes me sound like a parent," she says.

"Nothing you'll get any complaints about." I deadpan.

She drops into the chair on the other side of my desk. "I mean it, Deacon. You cause any issues and I'll—"

"Do what? I'm not going to harass her. I've known that woman since ... forever, and I won't do anything to hurt or upset her."

She gives me a short, sharp nod in response.

"But I might just marry her." I grin.

Rochelle shakes her head, seemingly fighting a smile. "Just be careful. I don't want you putting your own company at risk."

"I'm not about to do that. I also know there are no rules against staff fraternisation, and while there's a power imbalance between us, I'd never pressure Pippa into doing anything she doesn't want to. Hell, she's a grown woman who can make up her own mind."

Rochelle straightens up and nods. "That's a much better response."

"Pippa's always been dear to me. I'll make sure if either one of us has concerns, we talk to you."

That seems to satisfy her as she rises from her chair and walks toward the door. "She's nice. I like her."

"So do I."

———

"Knock knock."

Last night I kept thinking about today, and I didn't sleep that great. I'm not sure why the thought of seeing Pippa again makes me nervous—I practically lived at the Chapmans' sometimes. But grown-up Pippa is a very different prospect than the Pippa I knew back then.

For a distraction, I buried myself in reports this morning.

I look up and Pippa's gaze locks onto mine.

"Is it ten already?" I smile.

"Right on the dot."

I push myself up from my desk. "Prompt. I like it."

She beams a radiant smile at me. "I've been doing all the paperwork with Rochelle."

"So you're all set?"

Nodding, she walks into the room, and takes my breath away. She's wearing a black, knee-length skirt that hugs her curves. Her jacket's nestled in her arms, and her crisp, white blouse tucked into her skirt emphasises that hourglass figure.

Holy shit.

I'm not supposed to have this reaction to my ex-best friend's little sister, but it's all I can do to keep my jaw off the floor.

She tilts her head. "Deacon? Are you okay?"

I blink to break my stare. Her first day, and she's going to think I'm some kind of pervert. But this was not what I expected even after seeing her yesterday.

"I'm looking at you, Pip. You're gorgeous."

She blushes and slides her hand over her eyes. It's familiar, and

I'm taken back to the fun and laughter we all shared as kids—back before Lucas broke us.

I walk around the desk and remove her hand from her face.

"Deacon," she murmurs.

"Let's go and have coffee. I want to know all about your life." Giving her hand a squeeze, I guide her out of the room and to the elevator.

I'm well aware there are eyes on us, and when we reach the lobby, Pippa takes a deep breath.

"You okay?"

She nods. "It's a little overwhelming, but I'm fine. You did good, Deacon."

My chest swells a little at her praise. We've all worked hard at building this business—our revenue increases year on year as we get into new markets.

Two years ago, we moved into this multi-storey building which just highlights our growth. All five floors are ours, and there's a little coffee shop right in front which is handy for these moments.

It's busy, and we have to queue for a few minutes. I keep glancing at Pippa. She's clearly nervous, knitting her fingers together and biting her bottom lip.

"Order what you want. My shout." I smile.

"A flat white with one sugar," Pippa tells the barista.

"Make that two? Having here."

I grab a number, pay, and lead Pippa to a quiet booth down the back of the shop.

She slides into it while I keep my distance and sit on the other side.

"I still can't believe I'm here," she says. "If I'd known in the early stages the job was here ..."

"You might not have applied?"

She nods. "I was never sure how you'd react if we saw each other again."

I draw in a deep breath. This subject was always going to come up. How can we move forward, even if it's just friendship without addressing the past?

"Things were tough back then. I'd just found out about my mother, and I wasn't fair on you."

Pippa shakes her head. "No, you weren't."

Ouch.

She sucks on her top lip before continuing. "There's something I want to clear up—something you got wrong back then."

Double ouch.

"What is it?"

"Here's your coffee."

The cups are placed on the table, and I smile at the waitress and nod. "Thank you."

Pippa wraps her hands around her cup before she meets my gaze. "You thought I knew what was going on that day. I didn't. Lucas said he was going to your place, and my parents made him take me so I wasn't home alone."

I nod slowly. That day is a bit of a blur. One minute my dad and I were on our way to go fishing. The next, we were headed home because there was some work emergency. After he found Mum in bed with Lucas, they argued before he took off to deal with the work issue.

Then things got nasty between my mother and me.

"Lucas called you his lookout."

She shrugs. "I guess he was pissed at being caught. When we went there, I thought you were inside and that the two of you were just going to be playing games as usual. I had no idea you and your dad weren't there. I stayed outside to read my book. Your mother brought me a drink. I fell asleep on that seat."

My stomach sinks. I don't know what I said to her, but I do know I was angry—angrier than I've ever been in my life. For years, my parents fought, but I knew they loved each other—at least, I thought they did.

Mum had a real screwed-up idea of love.

"I'm sorry if I said anything to upset you, Pippa. I was a mess back then. You were a kid—even if you knew about Lucas and my mother, I wouldn't blame you if you said nothing." I blow out a long breath.

She reaches across the table and places her hand on mine. "I just always wanted you to know. You never gave me a chance to tell you."

"I was so young and stupid." I turn my hand up and squeeze hers. "What I do know is that I'm really glad you're here." Pulling back my hand to hold up my cup and take a sip, I shoot her a wink. "Now, tell me about you."

Her smile lights up her face. That's the Pippa I knew. That girl never had a care in the world. Her parents adored her, and Lucas for all his faults was a proud big brother—even when he was grumpy with her.

She was always sunshine even on the cloudiest of days.

"What do you want to know?" she asks.

I lean back in my seat. "The last time we saw each other ..."

Her brows knit, and I swallow hard. She probably doesn't want to remember that day any more than I do.

"It was twelve years ago, Pip. I'm sure a lot has happened in your life since then."

She shrugs and drops her gaze. "There's not a lot to tell. I finished high school, went to uni in Wellington, worked down there for a while, and now I'm here."

"What brought you to Auckland?"

Her head shoots up, and those hazel eyes fix on me. "Something different? I thought there'd be more opportunities here, and the chance to earn better money. The company I worked for in Wellington had gone into receivership, and I knew if I left it too late I'd be out of a job, so I took the initiative and planned my exit."

"You were always smart. Smarter than either me or Lucas."

Her affectionate gaze is unsettling—more than it should be. She was so soft-hearted, and she never held back when it came to telling people how she felt.

"I don't know about that. Look at everything you've built. You and your friends have done amazingly well. Your drinks are everywhere."

I nod. "Yeah, I'm really proud of that. I wish Dad was around to see it."

Her whole expression changes, and my heart lurches as I think I just broke hers. Tears well in her eyes. "Your dad isn't with us anymore?"

"You didn't know?"

She shakes her head, and I feel like the biggest bastard for dropping it on her like that.

"I'm not sure about the rest of my family, but I didn't hear anything about you *or* your dad after you left. It was too sad to talk about. I only knew about your success because your company was in the media. You made me so proud." She smiles through her tears, and I lean over and swipe a couple that have landed on her cheeks with my index finger.

"Don't cry. My dad wouldn't have wanted to make you sad. He thought you were the bee's knees. Just like I did."

Her lower lip wobbles, and before I can stop myself, I'm on the other side of the booth. I wrap my arm around her shoulder, and she leans into me. Closing my eyes for a moment, I breathe in the vanilla scent of her perfume.

"I'm so sorry, Deacon. Your dad was always so nice to me."

I know I shouldn't—not when she's technically on company time, but I kiss the top of her head and hold her close. "I'm sorry to tell you this way. I think he'd be happy we're working together."

She barks out a laugh. "I still don't know how that happened. Are you crazy?"

"Maybe just a little." I plant another kiss in her hair. Twelve years apart is too much. If I'd stayed, would this shift in how I'm feeling about her have taken place? We were all so close, but time apart has changed everything. "I don't want to let you go now. It's been too long."

"Then don't," she whispers.

"As much as I'd like that, we do have to get to work at some point." I chuckle, but the truth is I'm very reluctant to let her go now she's in my arms.

"Can we just stay here for a minute?"

I smile to myself. "Of course we can. I can't tell you how good it is to have you here."

"I'm just hoping I'm up to the task of keeping you in line." She pulls away a little and gazes at me, her eyes skimming over my face.

"Whatever you tell me to do, I'll do it."

Her cheeks pink up. This attraction isn't a one-way street.

"It's going to be that easy, huh?"

"When it comes to you? Yes."

Chapter Seven

Pippa

I'm confused, but happy.

Spending time with Deacon is everything I ever dreamed of—even if it's just taking half an hour out of his day to be with me.

Once we've finished our coffees, he escorts me back to the office.

Sitting at my new desk is a gorgeous blonde. Her hair's drawn up into a tight bun, and her makeup's on point. I might look together, but just laying eyes on her makes me feel disorganised.

She wasn't here when I came in before.

Her gaze falls on me, and I just know I'm being judged.

"Deacon. So nice of you to turn up for work."

He chuckles. "You know me so well, Simone."

Wait.

This is Simone? The PA who's been promoted to the CEO's office?

"You shouldn't be leading the poor woman astray on her first day." She busts out a big smile and meets my gaze. "I'm sorry. Here I am sitting in your seat. That's hardly welcoming."

When she stands, I feel even less confident. She could be a

model, she's so tall, and she has a figure to die for. I dress confidently, but I'm well aware of my inadequacies.

"Pippa, this is Simone, my former PA. Simone, this is Pippa."

She makes her way around the desk and holds out her hand. I give it a shake, and she closes her other hand over mine. "I'm so glad to meet you, and even more glad that he's your problem now."

Deacon reaches up and scratches the back of his neck. "This isn't awkward at all. It's like your girlfriend meeting your ex."

She laughs. "You should be so lucky. I'm sure Pippa has *much* better taste."

I snort.

He nudges my arm. "Hey, play nice."

My first impression of her was so off. I like this woman.

"I thought Simone could run you through the system today," Deacon says.

Simone holds a palm in the air and waves it. "I'll show her how I had things set up. Pippa can set up her own system. She can probably teach me a thing or two."

Oh, I *really* like this woman.

"If you say so." Deacon's bemused tone makes me smile. He turns to focus on me. "I'll get back to the reports I was working on this morning. Ladies." With a nod to Simone, he leaves us to go into his office, and she breathes a sigh of relief.

"Thank goodness he's gone. Now we can get down to the gossip."

I gawp. "Gossip?"

"The executives are all talking about you. I know you've known Deacon for years. And you're still putting up with him? That's messed up."

"He's not *that* bad."

She grins. "I know. Come on. I'll grab another chair and walk you through everything. I meant what I said about making changes. Do what works for you."

It doesn't take long to fall into easy conversation with Simone, and by the end of the day, I feel like I've made a friend.

Deacon heads out mid-afternoon for a meeting, and he hasn't returned by the time I finish. After our morning when I felt a connection with him, it's disappointing. But I'll be back tomorrow and so will he.

One of the best things about landing this job is the parking. It's ridiculously expensive in Auckland to pay for parking. And because I'm the PA to the CTO, my car's nice and close.

I scan the parks to find Deacon's. His car's not there so I'm guessing his meeting ran over, or he's just gone for the day.

After sliding into my driver's seat, I close my eyes for a second. Spending the day with Simone was taxing. There's not a huge amount I have to learn, but I do need to know where everything is. It's been a while since I've had that much information pumped into me in a single day.

She's keen to move on and start her new job, and I get it. At least I'm a fast learner, and I don't have to keep everything set up the way she had it.

It'll take some time, but I'll soon have the office running the way I want it.

The traffic this time of day is awful, but I make it back to the studio flat I'm renting before six and heat up leftovers from last night's roast chicken for dinner before sinking into the couch.

With a full stomach, and nothing to do but watch television, I'm nodding off before I know it. I'm even more tired than I realised.

I barely make it to 8.30 p.m. before climbing into bed.

My phone buzzes on the bedside cabinet.

Deacon?

I'd programmed his number into my phone today on Simone's advice. She said he never called her after hours, but it's better I'm prepared if he calls me needing something.

My stomach falls. What did I do wrong? Is he calling to tell me off?

I draw in a deep breath, and press *accept call.* "Hello?"

"Pippa? It's Deacon."

Heat traverses my body at the sound of his deep voice. I shouldn't feel this way—not when he's my boss. "Deacon?"

"I just wanted to check in on you because I didn't get to say goodbye today. How was your first day?"

I sigh and close my eyes. "It was good. Simone went through everything, and it all looks pretty straight forward."

He chuckles. "If anyone can keep me in line, it's you. I just wanted to say I'm really glad you applied for the job. I've missed you, Pip."

"I've missed you too," I croak.

"Are you okay?" His concerned tone does things to my stomach. The butterflies are back. I thought over time my crush on him had faded, but it's already back with a vengeance. I'm not sure if this is a good or a bad thing.

"I'm fine. Just tired. I didn't sleep too well last night, and today was a lot to take in." I bite my bottom lip. "I'm already in bed."

There's silence for a moment.

Have I overstepped?

"That worn out, huh? I hope that doesn't put you off working with me."

"Never." I laugh.

"Good to hear. Get some sleep, sweetheart, and I'll see you in the morning."

When the call is disconnected, I snuggle down into the sheets and smile. *Sweetheart.* I'm probably reading way too much into this, but I think Deacon sees me in a whole new light.

At least, I hope that's the case.

Chapter Eight

Deacon

Having Pippa in the office is unnerving.

I have to keep reminding myself I asked for this.

For the first few days, Simone flits back and forward between my office and Garrett's, picking up both her new work and passing hers onto Pippa. They seem to get on, so at least there's no dealing with jealousy and bitterness.

Pippa seems content to work for me instead of the CEO.

I do my best to steer clear of them while they're training. Neither of them need any more pressure from me, and everything's running smoothly, so I don't have any reason to be in their ears.

I'm content to watch Pippa from a distance. She's taking everything in her stride—always with a smile on her face. If nothing else so far, she's lightened the mood in my office.

But I'm not sure I'm that impressed at my team popping in to visit, which seems to happen much more often now she's here. Where I'm used to getting emails or even phone calls, I don't think I've had so many in-person visits since we started the company.

I can't blame them. Pippa dresses professionally, but those killer curves of hers can't be hidden.

She blossomed into a beautiful woman, and I've seen her in a whole new light.

It's driving me crazy.

At the start of the second week, she disappears at lunchtime rather than eating at her desk as she has been.

I give up stalking her and head down to the cafeteria. On Mondays, my friends can usually be found there. We all like to keep a hand in the business, making sure we're accessible to everyone. It helps prevent an 'us against them' mentality.

Mallory's nowhere to be seen, but Garrett and Victor sit in our spot and I give them a wave before grabbing today's lasagne special and heading to our table.

"How's it going?" Victor asks. "Pippa settling in well?"

I nod. "Seems to be. She's been with Simone a big chunk of this week, so we haven't had time to catch up."

"Come to check on her?" Garrett asks.

"Do I need to?"

He nods toward the corner of the cafeteria.

Pippa's surrounded by men. Her beaming smile lights up the whole room, and when she laughs, it's full and throaty and sends an unexpected signal to my dick.

Oh, hello.

I frown and growl before I realise I'm doing it.

Garrett and Victor laugh.

"You are so done for," Victor says. "I knew it was a bad idea hiring her to be your PA."

"It's not like you said anything." I turn back toward him.

"Did I say bad idea? I meant good idea. This is hilarious."

I glare at both of them before turning to watch Pippa.

"Simone's doing great, by the way. I'm glad you made that sugges-tion," Garrett says. "She says Pippa's settling in nicely. I think they'll work well together."

"That's good with the next product release coming up."

I nod. That's a very good point. Despite our size, organising product launches is an in-house affair. Mallory's in charge, but she would use Simone's organisational skills to help out. Having Pippa on board too is a real bonus for her.

It's usually a flashy evening event where we all dress up and have a good night out.

As Pippa's boss, it must be my job to escort her to her first work event.

"What's that smile about?" Victor asks.

"Nothing. Just thinking about work."

"Work or someone at work?" He teases.

"Do I need to be prepared to handle a complaint?" Garrett raises an eyebrow at me.

"Oh, come on, you guys. You know me better than that." I shovel a forkful of food in my mouth while they exchange a glance. I wait until I swallow and look at both of them. "I'd never hurt Pippa. But I might hurt one of them if they upset her."

Garrett snickers, and I roll my eyes, digging into my food and ignoring both of them.

Pippa's still in conversation with members of my team as I finish eating.

I stand and stalk toward her, ignoring the laughter behind me.

"I'm about to go up to the office. Are you having a long lunch?" I'm being a dick and I know it, but the last thing I need is another man stepping into my territory. And whether she knows it or not, Pippa is my territory.

She gazes up at me with wide eyes. "No. I'm just finishing up. See you back in the office?"

I give her a short, sharp nod and turn on my heel.

Garrett's red with laughter, and I glare at him as I make my way out of the cafeteria.

The poor elevator buttons bear the brunt of my irritation as I stab wildly at them, finally managing to make the damn things work on the third go.

By the time I've reached my office, I've cooled down a little, but

I'm acutely aware that I've also taken my temper out on the one person who's already had shit thrown at her. It took a lot for her to bring up *that* day, but she did because she didn't want me to think the worst of her.

What am I doing?

This woman has me twisted up in knots.

"Thanks for walking me back. It really wasn't necessary." Pippa's voice carries into my office, and my eyebrows rise.

"It's no problem," a distinctly male voice responds, and I'm on my feet before I know it. "I wondered if you'd like to go out sometime."

"Oh." Pippa's tone is neutral. "Well, uh, you see ..."

I take a handful of steps, not even sure what the hell I'm going to say to this guy to warn him off. Why am I warning him off? Pippa's not mine. I thought this whole *keep your friends close and your enemies even closer* thing made sense.

Pippa's no enemy.

She's a living, breathing work of art. The thoughts I'm having about her are far from brotherly.

"I've got a boyfriend," she says.

My lungs deflate, and I come to a stop. *What?*

I never asked her if she was seeing anyone. The idea of it makes me fist my hands.

"Oh. I'm sorry. I didn't realise."

"It's really serious. I think I'm going to marry him."

I start looking at the office wall, wondering which part is the best to punch.

"No worries, Pippa. I'll get going. Have a good rest of the day."

"You too," she sings.

The office is quiet, but for the sound of shuffling paper.

Pippa walks toward me.

Her head's down, and I stay still just waiting for the ...

She slams into my chest and looks up at me with wide eyes. "Sorry."

"In a hurry?"

Pippa shakes her head. "No. I got these finished before lunch but just wanted to go over them before I gave them to you. They're the IT reports consolidated." She manoeuvres around me and places them on my desk.

"Tell me about this boyfriend of yours."

When she bites her bottom lip, I suck in a breath.

"You heard that?"

My eyebrows rise. "Every word. Is it *that* serious?"

Her lips curl into a smile. "Very."

I'm not supposed to feel things for her, and this news is not supposed to make my heart sink. But it does.

"What's his name?"

She falters before steeling her spine. "Bob."

"Bob?" What kind of man calls himself Bob? Has she got a sugar daddy I don't know about? "When do I get to meet him?"

Pippa lets out a choked laugh. "I don't know if you ever will."

"Why not?"

Clamping her lips together, she shakes her head. "Are you jealous?"

I cock an eyebrow and lean in, my face inches from hers. "Why would I be jealous?"

"Because you're acting weird."

Reaching for her, I grasp her shoulders. "I'm just looking out for you. Who is this guy? Does he take good care of you?"

The snort that comes from her is baffling, and she pulls away, her hand over her eyes as she laughs. "Oh, he takes *very* good care of me."

"Damn it, Pippa. I care. Okay?"

She stops laughing, the expression in her eyes softening as she gazes at me. "It might not seem like it right now, but I appreciate you looking out for me."

I grab hold of her hand. "Always."

The gentle smile she gives me makes my heart pound. What is wrong with me?

"I'm sorry if you got the wrong idea at lunch, Deacon. I just thought if I spend time with your team that it might help me understand some of the things I have to work with. Simone said she did it."

Ugh. Her words just make me feel like an even bigger bastard.

"Simone isn't you. I don't care who she spends time with."

She swallows hard. "You're jealous?"

"Yes." There's no point in hiding it. I am jealous. I want her attention—all of it.

Reaching up, she cups my cheek. I fight a frown—is she going to let me down hard?

"If you want me to have lunch with you instead, I'll do it. I'd rather spend time with you anyway."

"Really?"

She has a boyfriend.

"I'd rather spend time with you than anyone else."

Chapter Nine

Deacon

I think I'm going mad.

I've pored over Pippa's social media for the past few days—she's on Instagram, and I've sent her a friend request on Facebook, and there's no sign of a boyfriend.

There are photos from her uni days of her with groups of people, and a couple of photos where she's with a particular guy I assume she was seeing at the time. But nothing matches what she was saying yesterday.

I'm neglecting my work, scrolling through endless photos and looking at captions.

"I'm just going for coffee," Pippa calls. "Want one?"

"Yes, please."

She appears in the doorway, a bright smile on her face. "I'll see what food they have too. Be back in a minute."

"Okay."

After she's gone, I study the empty doorframe for a moment. When I saw her photo on that application, I never anticipated *her*. While I thought it would be nice having her back in my life, I never foresaw myself having such strong feelings.

I don't want to mess this up.

"Deacon?" Mallory walks straight into my office. "Where's Pippa?"

"Gone for coffee."

She drops into the seat on the other side of my desk. "I wanted to ask for her help for organising this next product launch. I know it's not for another couple of months, but Simone helps out and an extra pair of hands would be great."

I nod. "If there's anything she can do, I'm sure she'd be happy to. Just as long as it doesn't interfere with her work."

"It won't." Malloy sucks on her bottom lip. "How are things going with you two?"

Snorting, I shake my head. "They're not."

Arching one eyebrow, she leans forward. "Really? I thought you'd be on the way down the aisle by now the way you pounced on her."

"I didn't pounce. I've been the perfect gentleman."

Mallory laughs. "I'm sure, but I thought you'd have made a move."

I pick up a pen and tap it on my desk. "She's got a boyfriend."

"No." Her expression straightens. "I'm so sorry, Deacon."

I shrug. "I'm still trying to find out about him. I overheard her telling one of the guys about him. It's serious too." I stab a piece of paper on my desk with the pen. "What kind of name is Bob anyway?"

Mallory slams her hand over her mouth, but her laugh still echoes around the room.

"What? What did I say?"

She shakes her head. "You know, for a modern man, you're not always that smart."

I narrow my eyes at her.

"Clearly, she's made up an excuse not to go out with this guy. I don't know why, but she's giving him the polite brush off instead of just saying no."

I frown. "Huh?"

"Go to the Urban Dictionary on your computer and look up Bob."

Giving her the side-eye, I pull the keyboard closer and do what she says. Nothing makes sense. I scroll down through the first couple of definitions before I hit ...

"No."

Mallory laughs. "Yes."

"Battery operated boyfriend. She's talking about her vibe—"

"I'm back." Pippa waltzes in the door, coffee in one hand and a bunch of bags in another. "They had those savoury muffins you like, so I grabbed a couple. Oh, hey, Mallory."

"Good morning, Pippa." Mallory stands and meets my gaze. "I'll leave you two to it."

Pippa's chewing on her bottom lip as she watches Mal walk away. "Uh oh. What did I do?" She places the cup holder on the desk and divides the food up between us.

"Take a seat."

Her face falls and she hesitates before dropping into the seat recently vacated by Mallory. "What's going on?" she asks.

"It's come to my attention ..." I know I'm being mean, but I want to see her face when she realises what I've been doing. "... I know who Bob is. Or rather *what* Bob is."

She snickers.

"Very funny, young lady."

Pippa bites her bottom lip and looks up at the ceiling. "You worked it out."

"Why did you make up that story to reject Matthew? You had *me* going there. I thought I had competition."

Her gaze shoots back to me, and her mouth hangs open.

I nod. "Pippa, we're both adults. There's something there that wasn't—couldn't be there before."

To my relief, she nods. "I made up the story because despite no being a complete answer, it's not always enough for some men."

My brows knit. "What do you mean?"

She drops her gaze to the floor. "I had a bad experience once with a guy in a bar who didn't want to take no for an answer."

In an instant, I'm around the desk and kneeling in front of her, placing my hands on the arms of the chair. "Please tell me that doesn't mean what I think it does."

Her eyes flicker and meet mine. "Oh, no." She places her hands on mine and squeezes. "After pestering me in the bar, he ... he followed me home and tried approaching me again. My flatmate at the time was a six-foot-three rugby player built of solid muscle. He dealt with it."

I breathe out a sigh of relief. "If anything had happened to you ..."

"That was three years ago. Since then, I've used the old boyfriend excuse. Still doesn't always work, but most guys back off."

"Most?"

She gives me a smile, a warm and genuine one that tugs at my heart. "I'm fine, Deacon. I appreciate you looking out for me."

"I'd have killed the guy."

Pippa cups my face in her hands. "I'm fine."

"I'm beginning to think I'm going to have to wrap you in bubble wrap."

Her laughter makes me smile, and she drops her hands.

"So, when do I meet Bob?" I make an extra-special effort to enunciate the word and take in the glorious sight of her cheeks going pink.

"No one meets Bob." She laughs again, leaning forward in her chair.

I meet her, pressing my forehead to hers. "I'd like to be the first. I'm sure we'd work together well."

Her breath hitches. "Deacon."

"Have dinner with me. Tonight."

She pulls away, her eyes searching mine. "Deacon ..."

"After work, go home and do whatever you need to do before we go out. I'll pick you up from there."

Pippa nods, a smile spreading across her lips.
This is it—our fresh start.
It doesn't matter what came before.
This amazing woman is stealing my heart—regardless of our past.
Could she really be my future?

Chapter Ten

Pippa

Half my wardrobe is on the bed.

We're just going to dinner—I'm hoping that's just the start. For so long I had this dream in my head that Deacon would fall madly in love with me and we'd live happily ever after.

I'm not so sure that's what will happen, but even going to dinner seems like a step in the right direction.

Eventually, I settle on a simple blue dress. It's not too tight or revealing—although something like that would be tempting—but it still shows off my best assets.

Is this a date?

I feel like I should know the answer to this, and yet uncertainty still hangs in the air. Deacon's showing all the signs of being interested, but he also seems interested in renewing our friendship. But then there are the things he's said to me, and the anger at me hanging out with other men.

My stomach twists.

Hopefully tonight will give me the clarity I want.

A knock stirs me out of my thoughts, and I rush to the door.

Deacon stands on the other side, and I could swoon just looking at him.

He's not dressed all that different from work in dress pants and a dress shirt, but he's not wearing a tie and his sleeves are rolled up, showing off his impressive forearms—my weakness.

I let out a sigh before I can stop it.

He smiles. "Hey. Are you ready?"

I nod. "Just let me grab my purse." Nerves eat at my stomach, but I make my way through the living room and grab what I need.

Deacon steps inside. "So, this is where you live?"

"It's not much, but it's mine."

He frowns. It's tiny, but in a big city it's what I could afford on my own. I did my time flatting with others in Wellington, and while it's still always an option here, I just wanted to be independent. My savings paid the deposit and the first few weeks while I was looking for work, but now I'm earning enough to stay here.

"You look beautiful by the way."

I don't need to check the mirror to know I'm blushing. "Thank you."

"Shall we?" He offers me his arm, and I take it.

"Where are we going?"

"It's a surprise."

He leads me out to his car. It's a late model Audi, and as I sink into the passenger seat, I let out a sigh. It's so much better than the old piece of crap that I inherited from Lucas. To be fair, Mum and Dad offered to upgrade it when I went to university, but I opted for them helping me out with the rent instead.

"I'm glad it's Friday. It's been a long week," I say.

Deacon shoots a glance at me as he pulls out into traffic. "I hope we're not overworking you."

I grin. "No. Not at all. It's great. I'm really looking forward to working with Mallory and Simone on this launch party. We've been getting on really well."

He relaxes back into his seat. "I'm glad to hear it. I knew you'd fit right in."

Before I know it, we're heading into the city and parking near the viaduct. It's Friday night, and the place is buzzing with people everywhere.

After we've exited the car, Deacon takes my hand in his and raises it to his lips. "They do the best pasta here. I hope you're hungry."

I grin. "Sounds great."

We walk toward the restaurant, and Deacon holds my hand tight. Excitement races through my veins. This is really it. I'm on a date with *Deacon Miller.*

But the excitement only lasts a short time.

"Mr Miller." A woman's voice rings out. The maître d' greets us with a warm smile before she gives me the once over.

Wait. They know him by name?

Does he come here that often?

Does he bring other women here?

As she leads us to the table, Deacon gives my hand a squeeze. "You're thinking," he whispers. "For what it's worth, I've had business lunches here but never brought a date. Only you."

I swallow hard.

"Right this way." She leads us to an intimate table in the corner.

My heart's racing. This is my idea of a romantic dinner, complete with candles on the table. My previous dates have always been much more casual, so I'm not sure I have much to compare it to, but it feels like Deacon's putting in the effort.

Deacon pulls my chair out, and I share a smile with him as I sit.

We're given the drinks menus, and he sits opposite me before giving them a quick look over.

A few moments later, we're joined by a waitress. "Can I get you anything to drink?"

Deacon looks at me, and I nod. "A glass of the house white?"

She smiles and shifts her gaze to him. "And for you, sir?"

"The same."

When she leaves, he reaches across the table and takes my hand in his. "You look nervous."

"We're on a date. I think. I'm trying not to freak out."

His grin brings a smile to my face. "*You're* trying not to freak out. How do you think I feel?"

"What do you mean?"

Deacon laughs. "From the moment you walked into my life, this is all I've thought about. And now you're here. Thank you for coming out with me tonight."

I shrug. "Could I really refuse?"

"What do you mean?"

My heart thuds. It's now or never. His gaze is fixed on me, and it's unnerving, and my stomach's still churning. But I have to go for it. "I've had a crush on you my whole life. Why would I ever say no to dinner with you?"

A smile plays on his lips. "You did?"

His reaction slows my heart rate. At least he's not freaking out.

"Ever since you rescued Roger from the tree."

Deacon chuckles. "How old were you?"

"Five, I think?"

He shakes his head. "I had no idea."

Growing more confident, I laugh. "I'm glad because I would have been mortified back then if you knew."

His smile's warm, but when he doesn't respond, the nerves begin to grow again.

"Here are your drinks."

Our wines are placed on the table, and I give the waitress a tight smile. It's not her fault that her timing sucks.

"Can you give us a few more minutes to read the menu?" Deacon asks.

"Sure thing." She's so bright and bubbly, and I hate that I resent her right now.

As soon as she's gone, he puts all his focus back on me, and it's like there was no gap in the conversation.

"Seven years was a big difference back then. It's not really that much now," he finally says.

My throat tightens.

"I want this, Pippa. I want to explore *us*."

He meets my gaze again, and there's a question in his eyes.

He's waiting for me to agree.

"I'd like that." I'm breathless with excitement. This is Deacon. I never forgot him—I couldn't. Losing him from my life was the worst thing that ever happened to me.

"I'd really like to kiss you, but I'm not sure the restaurant would appreciate it if I dived across the table to do it." He grins.

I laugh, but my heart swells and all I can think about now is us kissing.

"Thank you for saying yes to dinner, Pippa." He holds up his wine glass. "I'd like to think this is just the start."

I clink my glass with his for his toast.

"Let's check out this menu."

———

It's the best pasta I've ever eaten in my life.

When I choose the chicken carbonara, Deacon follows suit, reassuring me that even though he hasn't tried it, everything on the menu is good.

We settle into easy conversation. We might not have been a part of each other's lives for years, but apart from the obvious topic—nothing's off limits.

I haven't felt so comfortable with anyone in a long time.

"I'm so full." I lean back in my seat and rest my hand on my stomach. "This was a wonderful idea."

"Too full for dessert?"

"Never."

Deacon barks out a laugh. "That's my girl. They do a mean tiramisu here."

"Ohhh, I love tiramisu."

"I want to know all about the things you love." His eyes search mine. "I want to give you the world, Pippa. All I need is to know where to start."

"You're starting just fine from where I'm sitting."

For a moment, we just gaze at each other, until Deacon breaks away.

"Fuck dessert. I want to take you home and kiss the crap out of you."

It's my turn to laugh, and I shake my head.

"It's too late, Mister. I want my tiramisu."

"Can we get it to go?"

I raise my index finger to my chin and give it about two seconds of thought.

"You bet we can," I say softly.

Because there's nothing better right now than the thought of Deacon kissing the crap out of me.

I've never seen that man move so fast as he orders my dessert, and before I know it, we're hauling arse down the motorway toward my flat.

And if I thought my heart raced before—that was nothing.

Every step toward my front door is agonising, and when we reach it, I turn and take in the sight of this man—this man I've dreamed about for so long, and I take a deep breath.

"Do you want to come in?"

His eyes search mine.

Please say yes.

"I think you know I do."

After unlocking and opening my door, I step in with him on my heels.

"Do you want a drink or something?"

Deacon captures my hand and pulls me toward him.

"I'll take or something."

I fight my smile, but I can't help it. "Is that right, Mr Miller?"

"You know how I feel, Pippa." He kicks the door closed.

I step backward, and he follows until we reach the couch.

He chuckles as I sit before taking a seat right next to me.

"I don't know where to start with you. Since you walked back into my life, I've wanted you."

My mouth goes dry, and I have to lick my lips to be able to speak. But even then, words don't come out.

His gaze drops to my lips. "Now you're just teasing."

I laugh. "I'm really not, I ..."

Deacon leans in, and his lips are inches from mine. "I told you at the restaurant that I wanted to kiss you. But, Pippa, you really have no idea what you do to me."

"Kiss me, then?"

My heart pounds out of my chest when his lips touch mine. He starts soft and gentle, before I open for him.

And then it's on. He plunders my mouth as if it's the last time we'll ever kiss.

When he finally pulls away, he leans his forehead on mine.

"God, Pippa. You're perfect."

He runs his hand down my spine, and I shiver at his touch. This is it. This is the moment I dreamed of for so long. It's here, and it's real, and it's everything.

His eyes search mine. I've seen so many emotions in this man, but now all I see is his affection for me.

"I'm not sure about that." I try and lighten the mood.

"I am. And I don't want to wait another moment to kiss you again."

"Go on."

His lips meet mine, and I'm done for. It only takes a second for him to deepen the kiss, and before I know it, his tongue's in my mouth and I'm letting out a moan that I've never heard come out of me before.

What is even happening right now?

His hand rests on my hip, much to my frustration. I know this is the first time we've been out together, but I want more.

I want everything.

He keeps on kissing me, occasionally letting me up for air, but there's so much promise in it.

"I love kissing you," he whispers. "But I'm going home."

I bite my bottom lip. Tonight I took a chance that paid off. Can I make it two for two?

"You don't have to."

Deacon's lips curl into a smile. "Maybe not, but I'm going to. It's not that I don't want to stay, but I want to do this properly. Tonight's been a revelation."

I peck him on the lips. "I hope I didn't freak you out."

He shakes his head. "No. I feel like when I saw your photo that my eyes were opening for the first time. You're too important to me to rush this."

Oh, my heart.

He grabs my hand and brings it to his chest. "I want you, Pippa. Maybe more than I should. I can't forget our past, but I'd like to think we can build a foundation for a future."

It's as if this man just walked out of one of my books. Teenage Deacon was hot—adult Deacon is on a whole other level.

He lingers at the door, kissing me softly.

"It's too tempting to stay. You're too tempting."

"See you on Monday?"

Deacon kisses me again. "Wouldn't miss it for the world. Make sure you lock the door when I've gone."

"I will."

"Goodnight, Pippa."

I close the door and lock it before turning and leaning against it. Letting out a contented sigh, I can't wipe the grin from my face.

I'm not sure where this is going, but it feels so good.

———

The next date, two days later, is the same.

He takes me for a nice dinner, and afterward kisses me senseless before leaving.

I know what he's doing—we're both trying to be patient. I've never been one to rush into anything, but with Deacon all I want to do is rush.

The way he struggles to pull away from me, I get the feeling Deacon's the same.

But no matter what's happening between us, I'm walking around with a near permanent smile on my face. I never dreamed Deacon would return my feelings.

"So, are you seeing Deacon now?" Mallory asks.

I nod. "We've been on a couple of dates."

She presses her lips together and places her hand on my arm. "Just … be careful."

Frowning, I tilt my head. "What do you mean?"

Mallory hesitates before answering. "He's my friend, but he's not good with commitment. In all the time I've known him, he's not been in a relationship. He's not that good with them."

I straighten up and swallow hard. "Well, we're different."

Her smile's forced. "I'm sure you are."

I've liked Mallory up until today. Now, I'm not so sure.

"I've known him all my life, Mallory. I know I'm safe with him."

"Even after your brother screwed him over?"

I'm not one to lose my temper, and I'm not dumb enough to lose it at one of the company owners. But I'm not taking this lying down. "What happened is in the past, and between them. It's got nothing to do with me."

She holds her palms up as if surrendering. "Okay, but don't say I didn't warn you. He's not one for girlfriends or sticking with one woman for very long. I'm just trying to protect you."

"I don't need your protection."

We're nearly finished with planning the invitations for the launch, and I'm only a few minutes from going to lunch before I return to my desk for the afternoon.

Mallory gives me a short, sharp nod, and I'm gone.

But her words echo in my brain.

Is she right?

Chapter Eleven

Deacon

Walking away from Pippa at the end of the night is getting tougher and tougher.

It's taking every ounce of control I have not to pounce on her the second I get her alone.

But I want to show her that I'm a good man—one who's not just after her for sex. If I get this right, we'll have a lifetime together.

It's also way too early to be thinking like that, but from the moment Pippa walked back into my life, I was a goner.

So, the other reason for holding back is because I don't want to freak her out.

She's told me all about her crush on me, but that was a long time ago and we were both kids.

Tonight is different. Tonight is when I make my move because I don't just want Pippa on my arm, I want her in my bed.

She hasn't been to my place before, so I'm pulling out all the stops.

I'm going to wine and dine her, and ask her to spend the night with me.

The ghosts of our past still linger—I can't pretend they don't.

Lucas betrayed our friendship, and that had a devastating impact on my family. It wasn't just Mum and Dad. Words were said that broke me at the time.

I'm still not sure how I navigate through that, but for Pippa's sake, I have to try. Lucas will be a part of her life no matter what, but I'm head over heels for his sister now, which I never saw coming.

I do my best not to clock watch, but it's hard when all I want is to be with her. We both left the office at five, so we're eating a little later than usual to give her time to go home and get ready. Not that I wanted her to.

I wanted to take her home and never let her go.

But in typical Pippa fashion, it's right on seven when she arrives.

I take a deep breath before opening the door, and she's right there with a big smile on her face. Before my nerves get the better of me, I draw in close, wrap an arm around her waist, and pull her into the room.

"Hi."

Her breath quickens. I'm not sure if she knows what I have planned tonight, but she must suspect.

"Hi," she replies.

"I'm glad you're here."

"Me too?"

Her brow furrows, and I know I need to pull myself together. I'm not sure why I'm so nervous.

"Deacon, you're acting weird again."

I lean down a little to kiss her, and she sighs when I finally let her free.

"That's more like it." She pats my chest. "What's for dinner?"

I'm lost in her eyes for a moment, and I blink rapidly to pull myself out of it. "What? Oh, I'm cooking a stir-fry with chicken and vegetables."

Pippa walks toward the stovetop before picking up a wooden spoon and giving the food a stir. "That smells amazing."

I bury my nose in the back of her neck. She leans against me and sighs.

"You smell amazing."

Her peels of laughter make me smile. She's the same as she always was, kind and caring, and also full of laughter. Even when she was younger, Pippa's laugh could change the mood in a room.

"I also figured you'd be on time because you're always so prompt, so it's ready. We'll eat in the living room if you want."

"Sounds great." She turns and pecks me on the lips. "I'll let you do your thing."

"Oh, I'm doing my thing tonight. I promise."

Pippa laughs and shakes her head.

"And if you're a good girl, you might even get tiramisu for dessert."

Her mouth falls open. "No way."

"Yes. Now get over to that couch before I burn dinner and you leave me."

———

After dinner and a glass of wine, I lean back on the couch and gaze at my girl.

"Stay with me tonight."

My invitation floats in the air as she gives me a shy smile.

I've never been so nervous. Since I hit puberty, I've been so confident with women, but Pippa's different.

She's the one that really matters.

"I'll stay," she whispers.

I gather her in my arms and kiss her hard.

"Come with me." Taking her hand, I lead her into the bedroom. "Gonna need you naked, Pip."

Her eyes widen, and colour floods her cheeks. She's not shy, but there's something else holding her back and I'm not sure what it is.

"I ... I mean. Umm." She's so cute when she's flustered.

I reach for the top button of my shirt, and she watches silently as I move from one button to the next until I tug open my shirt. She licks her lips when I slide it down my arms and let it drop the floor while never taking my eyes from her face.

"Your turn."

"Deacon, I ..."

Reaching out, I cup her cheek. "You're so beautiful, princess. And I want to see you."

She gives me a curt nod, and I reach for the hem of her shirt before lifting it over her head. Her breasts are encased in white lace, the darker nipples prominent through the fabric.

Pippa gulps.

"God, Pippa. You're even more gorgeous than I imagined."

"You really think so?" she whispers.

I rest my hands on her breasts, giving them a gentle squeeze. "You have no idea how much I've fantasised about these."

Her soft laugh makes me smile.

I know she worries about her weight—I've heard her talking to Mallory about dieting, but she's all lush curves and delectable flesh. I've been itching to get my hands on her, and now I have to take it slow or I'm afraid I'll freak her out.

Taking her by the hand, I lead her to my bed.

I'm so deep already with this woman. Tonight will be my final downfall.

She reaches for my belt, and I hold my hands out of the way, letting her unbuckle it and drop my pants to the floor.

Her chest rises and falls, and I reach for her again, holding the back of her head while I kiss her hard, her soft breasts pressed against my chest. I let go of her long enough to unhook her bra, dragging the straps down her arms and throwing it across the room.

Pippa laughs, her hands already on the waistband of my boxers.

"I want you," I whisper.

"I'm yours," she replies. "There's something you should know."

My eyebrows rise. "What is it?"

"It's just ..." She bites her bottom lip, and it's maddening. "I don't have a lot of experience, and I'm not like the other women in your life."

My eyebrows rise. "Other women?"

"You know. Like the women I've seen you with on your social media."

I shake my head. "My social media is usually work related. It doesn't reflect my taste in women."

Her brows knit. "I thought ... What is your taste in women?"

"You."

She giggles when I lunge at her, burying my face in her neck and nibbling at the junction where it meets her shoulder. "Deacon, be serious."

I raise my head. "I am serious. You're my taste. And if I don't get to taste you soon, I'll go crazy."

A smile spreads across her lips. "I don't know what to do when you talk like that." She pushes me down onto the bed.

"When did you get to be so bossy?"

"When I realised there's one thing I think I'm good at. You'll have to let me know."

Her shy smile is driving me insane, but its's clear she's out of her comfort zone now and just going for it.

"You can do to me whatever you want to, sweetheart."

"I was hoping you'd say that."

She drops to her knees, and the sight is enough to make me lose it on the spot.

After hooking her fingers back around the waistband of my boxers, she tugs them down my legs until I'm bared completely to her.

This isn't how I pictured this going. I wanted to unwrap her like a present and savour her nakedness before giving her more orgasms than she's ever had.

All I can do instead is gape as she wraps her hand around my hard cock and strokes it.

Holy shit.

I think I died and went to heaven.

But that's nothing compared to the moment she takes me in her mouth and her wet heat rolls down me.

Her mouth—her mouth is like silk, and she starts up a rhythm that has my eyes rolling in my head.

"Oh good God, Pippa, you're so good at that. Oh, baby."

She responds by tightening her grip, her other hand cupping my balls. If I thought how she started was good, it's nothing compared to this.

I reach for her, careful not to push her down but sliding my hand around the back of her head. It's taking all my control not to just fuck her mouth hard, but I want her to drive this.

She picks up the pace, and with every stroke I thank my lucky stars for her being in my life again. And I already know I never want her to share this with any other man.

She's my girl.

"Shit, Pip. I'm coming."

If I thought she'd let up, I was wrong. Sensation washes over me as she takes me over the edge, and I blow into her mouth.

Finally, she lets go and looks up.

She meets my gaze and swallows. It's the sexiest thing I've ever seen.

"I thought ... I don't know what I thought because my brain's not working right now," I get out.

Pippa laughs gently.

"Where did you ... No. I don't want to know."

She rises slowly, and I cup her face.

"That sweet mouth is all mine from now on."

"Deacon," she whispers.

"Lie on the bed. I want to see you."

With a laugh, she climbs up behind me, and I turn my head in time to see a glimpse of her white-lace-covered arse before she drops down on the bed and rolls over.

She crosses her arms over her chest, and I shake my head.

"Not a chance. I want to see *you*."

I crawl over top of her and sit astride her thighs.

Reaching for her hands, I pull them apart. She's so beautiful, her full creamy breasts on display with those darker pink nipples. She tries to slide her hands over her stomach, but I stop her.

"Deacon, I—"

"You are gorgeous. You're everything I ever dreamed of."

Her eyes search mine.

"Pippa. Relax. You're with me, and I love every single thing about you."

The flush of her cheeks is endearing—she's nearly naked, but it's not enough. I need to see all of her.

I slip my hands into her panties, and after a moment she nods.

After tugging them down her legs, I drop them to the floor before getting back onto the bed. "Tuck your legs up."

Her sharp intake of breath tells me just how nervous she is.

"Pippa. I need to taste you, baby. Give me your pussy."

Pippa's eyes widen, but she pulls her legs up. I place my hands on her trembling knees and push them apart, exposing her. She's so pretty and pink with her pubic hair tightly trimmed.

"Jesus, Pippa."

She gasps and tries to pull her knees together. I hold up a palm.

"No, sweetheart. You're just so ... perfect. I can't wait any longer."

As she relaxes, I slide down onto my stomach until I'm face to face with her perfect pussy. I'm suddenly starving—like a man who hasn't eaten in forever. And all I want is her.

She gasps again as I touch her, exposing her clit and teasing it with my tongue.

"I'm just returning the favour, sweetheart. That blow job was monumental."

I raise my head as she laughs, loving how her full breasts jiggle in time with it.

I'm so in love with her.

Grasping her hips, I pull myself in and feast. She squirms under my tongue, her breath quickening when I suck on her clit.

And I don't stop until she shudders underneath me, calling out my name.

"Pippa, do I need a condom?"

Her chest heaves like she's just run a marathon. "I'm on the pill."

"I haven't been with anyone for nearly a year. And I was clear my last check-up."

She nods. "I trust you. I really just want you inside me."

"I want nothing more right now, sweetheart."

After crawling up the bed beside her, I roll onto my back and beckon her with my index finger. "Come here."

She straddles my waist, lowering herself onto my aching cock. I blow out a long breath as her tight heat engulfs me.

"Are you okay?" Her eyes are wide as if she's scared she's hurt me. "I know I'm a bit heavy."

"You're perfect." I run my hands up the sides of her torso before cupping her breasts. "This is perfect. You feel amazing."

"You make me feel full." She laughs that throaty laugh, and I swear my cock gets harder.

"Close your eyes, beautiful," I murmur. "Just feel me."

Her eyelids slowly lower, and I pinch her nipples, making her smile.

Pulling her down toward me, I suck a nipple into my mouth, followed by the other one.

Pippa grinds against me, her breathing erratic. Sliding my thumb between us, I rub her clit until her eyes pop open and she lets out a low moan.

"That's it, baby. I want to see you come this time."

She arches her back.

Pippa doesn't see it in herself, but she's perfection.

I grasp her hips again, pulling her down hard, and rock my hips up to meet her. She leans over, her clit rubbing against the base of my cock.

"Oh yeah. Use me to get yourself off. Fuck, that's hot."

She meets my gaze, her eyelids fluttering as she fights the urge to close her eyes.

"Come with me, Pippa."

Her mouth opens, and she raises her arms to flick her hair back over her shoulders.

Running my hands up to her breasts, I knead them as a smile graces her lips.

And then she lets out a moan that goes to my toes—my body reacting as I rise to meet her again and come so hard I see stars.

As she slows, she leans over and kisses me, her soft lips caressing mine.

"That was amazing," she whispers.

"That—" I grin before kissing her again. "That was just the start."

Chapter Twelve

Pippa

What am I doing?

Last night was amazing—everything I ever dreamed of. But this morning, in Deacon's warm bed, I'm not sure anymore. Will he still want me now? Was the goal just to get me into bed? What is this between us?

I'm a raging inferno for him. Despite the past, I've been sucked back into this man's vortex and I've let myself be free. But was that a good idea?

I know I'm prone to overthinking but even now as I'm snuggled down in Deacon's arms, doubt penetrates my thoughts.

Raising the duvet, I wriggle out from underneath it. As my feet touch the ground, a large, warm arm wraps around my waist and pulls me backward.

"Where do you think you're going?" he rasps in my ear.

"I ... I ..."

"Come back here. I'm not finished with you." He plants kisses on my bare shoulder.

My eyelids flutter and I lean against him.

"Lay down with me. I'm having you for breakfast."

I laugh as I lie down and his hand trails down my leg. "Deacon."

"I love it when you say my name."

His blue eyes suck me in as his fingers get closer and closer to the spot I want him to touch. I roll my hips, and a smile crosses his lips.

"I love it when you touch me," I whisper.

He slowly drags his index finger over my clit. "Touch you like that?"

I nod.

"I love touching you."

His fingers make light work of my orgasm, and while I'm still floating, he rolls over and slides into me.

"You and me. We're good together. And I have every intention of being with you for as long as you want me."

I even my breathing out before answering, "Forever, then?"

Deacon's lips curl into a smile. "Sounds good to me."

This time, he slows everything down. His kisses are tender, and he loves my breasts, nuzzling and licking my nipples while he moves inside me.

I want this. I want it all the time with him.

I've never been one to move fast, but this just feels right. Maybe the fact that I've loved him for years has altered my perspective but being with Deacon is everything I ever hoped for.

"You feel so good," he moans before that final thrust and he collapses, resting his head between my breasts.

I love you.

It's on the tip of my tongue, but I want him to be the first to say it.

He rolls off me and lies on his back before rolling toward me and reaching for my hand.

"Where were you going this morning?" he asks.

I bite my bottom lip. "Home."

His brows pinch. "Sneaking off without saying goodbye?"

Nodding, I try and avoid his eyes but it's just too hard. "I wasn't sure if you would want me to hang around."

"Where did you get that idea?"

The intensity of his gaze makes me shrink back. "I ... someone told me you weren't one for relationships. She said—"

"Who said?" His voice is calm but his left eyebrow twitches, his annoyance right under the surface.

"Mallory." It's barely a whisper, but he hears because his anger flares for just a moment in his eyes before the softness reappears.

"She's Garrett's ex, and she looks out for all of us. Sounds like she got a little over-zealous. Probably to protect you."

"Do I need protecting?"

He grins. "Not in the way she thinks you do."

I bark out a laugh.

"I'm crazy about you, Pippa. There is no one else. Mallory's made me out to be worse than I really have been." He sighs, running his thumb down my cheek. "I can't deny there have been women in the past, but none who I've had this connection with. It sounds messed up because I've known you since we were kids, but I feel like I've been waiting my whole life for you."

Tears well in my eyes, and I smile through them because is what I've always wanted to hear. My heart's gone from being so empty to full as his words wash over me. "I'm sorry I doubted you."

"I don't know what this is between us, but I want it so badly. You, me, endless nights in my bed. Spending days together. All of it."

I swallow hard. "That's what I want too."

He smiles. "How about I make us breakfast and then we have a lazy day together?"

"That sounds perfect."

Chapter Thirteen

Deacon

One lazy day turns into another.

Apart from a brief period where Pippa dashed home to get clothing for work, we spent the whole weekend together.

And my heart feels whole for the first time in a long time.

Things between us are better than ever—not that I have much to compare it to, but I can see this lasting.

I haven't told her just how much that time period after Dad caught Mum in bed with Lucas messed me up. My relationship with my father intensified—we grew closer than ever, which made it all the harder when he died. But my mother messed with my head, and I still struggle with trusting people even now.

If I can protect Pippa from that, I will. The last thing I need is her doubting the way I'm feeling. Now she's told me she knew nothing about what was going on back then, I feel more confident with her.

She wanted to take her car this morning, but I know that car. It's the one Lucas got when he was sixteen. I'm not sure why Pippa's still driving around in the heap of junk, but she won't be for much longer if I can help it.

Instead, I insist that we travel in my car. She'll be safer, and I want her with me. I also don't care who knows about us. If they have an issue, they can take it up with me.

I don't miss her intake of breath as we pull into my car park.

"You okay?"

Pippa nods. "Just nervous all over again arriving with you."

Leaning over, I give her a tender kiss. "It'll be fine. Trust me."

After stepping out of the driver's seat, I walk around the car. I open the passenger door and take her hand.

She blushes and grins. "Thank you."

Keeping hold of her hand as she steps out, I push the door closed and use my fob to lock the car. "Come on."

She tugs her hand out of mine—or tries to, but I hold on tighter.

As we approach the front door, her breathing quickens. "I'm not sure—"

I squeeze her hand. "I'm making a public statement. I want the world to know that we're together."

Her hazel eyes widen in surprise. "I thought you'd want to keep it quiet."

Shrugging, I raise her hand to my lips and place a kiss on the back of it. "I'm not hiding anything. There's no company rule against us having a relationship."

Pippa tenses as we enter reception. Every head turns and the whispering is blatantly obvious in the usually quiet area.

I tug her hand so she's even closer. And I'm glad to see Mallory at the reception desk, her eyes glued on us.

"Morning." I grin.

Her gaze flicks down to our joined hands and back. "Morning."

We come to a stop, and I turn to Pippa. "Go on up to the office. I'll grab a couple of coffees and be there in a few."

Pippa nods. Her smile seems forced, but she holds it together.

I'm barely keeping my temper in check, but I can't let her see how Mallory's attempt to derail us is pissing me off. With another kiss to her hand, I let her go, and watch her all the way to the elevator.

"What's your problem?" I turn my gaze back to Mallory, and she sets her jaw.

"What do you mean?"

She walks off in the direction of the coffee shop, and I trail along behind her. Pippa's insecure enough without Mal getting in her ear about me.

Once our orders are placed, she heads toward a quiet corner of the shop.

"What do you want, Deacon?" She plants herself into a seat and glares at me across the table.

Oh, you know what you did.

"I wondered if we might have a word." The chair scrapes across the floor as I pull it out, but I'm too wound up to care.

I'll give her credit. She leans back in her seat and presses her fingertips together as if I've got a proposal for her to consider. "Regarding?"

"Why you tried to make Pippa believe I couldn't possibly be interested in more with her."

She rolls her eyes. "She's a lovely girl, but she's so young."

"There are only seven years between us. And she's mine now."

Her eyes flash with irritation.

But before she can say anything further, I hold up my hand. "Pippa and I are together now. Just so you know. Whatever stunt you were trying to pull is done." I stand and turn back toward the coffee pick-up.

"Deacon?"

I pause before looking back over my shoulder. "What?"

"I was just trying to protect her. I've known you for the past ten years, and—"

"Pippa's known me longer than you have. She knows me and she trusts me. What she doesn't need is someone feeding into her insecurities."

Mallory flinches as if she's been hit. "I'm sorry."

"Apologise to her." I stalk away, and when my coffee order's called, I grab the cups and make my way up to my office to see my girl.

My girl.

Now we're together, nothing and no one will take her away from me.

———

It's midmorning by the time I get to speak with Pippa again after dropping off the coffee earlier. The rest of the morning's been full of dealing with issues—nothing major, but there are always those pesky little things that crop up, and right now I've got my web designer working on a new concept for our website.

When I get back into my office, Pippa's sitting at her desk. Her expression is strained, and I hate it.

"Are you okay?"

Pippa rubs her temple. "I'm fine."

Shaking my head, I lean over the other side of her desk, propping myself up on my elbows and studying her. "I know what that means. If it's about Mallory, I took care of that."

One of Pippa's eyebrows dips. "I hope you didn't get me offside with her. She's still management."

Reaching for her hand, I raise it to my lips and brush a kiss over her knuckles. "She was looking out for you. But I made it clear that you're no one-night-stand for me."

Her lips wobble, and for a moment I think she's going to burst into tears.

"Thank you. But it's not what's giving me a headache."

"Oh?"

I scoot around the side of her desk until I'm standing behind her. On her screen is a website full of evening dresses.

She scrambles to place her hands over the monitor, but I reach for them, pulling them down so I can get a better look. "Is this for the release party?"

"Yes," she mumbles. "I was talking with a couple of the women in product development, and they told me it's a good excuse to dress up. But I don't really have anything that works."

I scan the screen. "Are you ordering online? I'll pay."

Pippa shakes her head. "I was going to the store at lunchtime. And you don't have to pay."

Leaning my head against hers, I pop a kiss on her temple. "I'll come with you."

"Deacon." She laughs. "Really? You want to come shopping with me?"

I shrug. "You're my girlfriend. Those dresses are sexy as fuck. You bet I want to see you try them on. I'll buy every one if I have to."

Her eyes are wide as she stares at me. What the hell did I say?

"I'm your girlfriend?"

I probably shouldn't kiss her in the office, but her lips are inches from mine and she's irresistible. My gaze stays fixed on hers as I cover the gap and give her a tender kiss. "What do you think you are after our weekend together?"

Pippa's smile is all I need to get me through the day. "I just hadn't thought of it in those terms."

"Well, get used to it. And schedule us both out of the office for a couple of hours around lunchtime because we have an appointment with a dress shop."

Her laughter follows me into my office, and I could eat out on it for days.

My life couldn't be sweeter. I've got the girl of my dreams, and everything's better than it has been, well, ever.

She's all I need.

When it hits midday, I head out to her desk and wait while she grabs her bag.

"You're seriously coming with me?" she asks.

"Hell, yes." I offer her my arm, and she takes it.

After a ten-minute walk, we reach the store, and as soon as I step in, I know I'm out of my depth.

I've never been shopping for women's clothing before.

Pippa moves between the racks before picking out two dresses. I see a flash of colour before she turns to me. "There's a bench over there by the changing room. You wait there and I'll try the first one on."

"Okay."

She hands me her bag. "Look after this."

"Love it when you're bossy." I grin.

She laughs then stalks toward the changing room, and I take a seat where she's told me to.

The bell rings above the door, and Mallory walks in.

She walks toward me, eyebrows raised. "What are you doing here?"

Her bemused look makes me smile.

"Helping my girlfriend buy a dress. I guess you're here for the same thing?"

She drops down onto the bench beside me. "You guessed right."

"You don't look so happy about it either."

Mallory laughs. "I hate this side of things. But I know I have to—"

I frown as she just cuts off, but then I turn my head and my mouth falls open. My woman is a goddess.

It's a simple black dress, but it hugs her curves and accentuates that cleavage I adore.

"Turn around." My voice is hoarse, and Mallory nudges my arm.

The back dips with black straps criss-crossing so she's not completely bare. It's nothing fancy, but she takes my breath away in all its simplicity.

"We are so buying that," I say.

Pippa turns around and her brows knit. "Are you sure? I thought it might be too tight."

"You look lovely," Mallory says. "It's perfect for the occasion. Dress it up with some strappy sandals and jewellery."

"What she said," I say. "Where's the next dress?"

Pippa laughs. "I'm just buying one."

I shake my head. "Nuh huh, I want to see you in both of them."

With a smile, she stalks back to the changing room.

"I was wrong," Mallory says.

Turning toward her, I frown. "About what?"

"You are good for her. And she's good for you. I'm sorry. I really was just trying to look out for her."

With a nod, I shift my gaze to the changing room. "I'm so crazy about her."

"I've never seen you like this before."

I shrug. "I've never felt like this before. She's the one."

Mallory grips my shoulder before rising from the seat. "I guess I should go and look for my own dress rather than watch you two."

"If you're quick, I'll give you my opinion." I grin.

She gives me a soft slap around the head. "I'm beginning to think there's something wrong with you."

"It's what love does, Mal."

Mallory rolls her eyes and takes off into the store.

The changing room door opens, and Pippa steps out. I catch my breath.

This dress is longer. It's dark red with a plunging neckline and hugs Pippa's hips like she was born to wear it. The hemline's below the knee, but there's a split up the side that stops just short of her panty line.

Holy shit.

"That's it. That's the one."

Pippa smiles. "Are you sure?"

"I want the other one too, but this is the dress for the launch party. You look beautiful."

Her cheeks flush with colour, and I rise to my feet, closing the gap between us.

"*You* are beautiful."

"Deacon ..." she murmurs.

"I'm serious. God I ..." I stop myself before I tell her I love her.

We've been together five minutes. The last thing I want to do is scare her off. But it's how I feel. I'm head over heels for her.

"You ...?" Her right eyebrow rises.

"I just ... you look incredible. Let's get both of them and get to work. I've got an errand to run this afternoon, but I'll be back for my later meetings."

Pippa frowns. "There's nothing in the calendar."

"I know. I just have to take care of something. So let's get out of here." I pop a kiss on her nose, and she screws it up as if she knows I'm full of it. But seeing her in that dress gave me an idea that she'll love and hate all at the same time, and I want to show her just how much she means to me.

"Okay." She pecks me on the cheek and disappears back into the changing room.

Mallory races into the cubicle next to her, and I sit down.

This is still going to take a while.

Chapter Fourteen

Pippa

I'm not sure why I have an apartment anymore.

When I'm not at work, I'm at Deacon's. And I'm not complaining. It feels like he's finally caught up to where I am. I've loved him for so long, it's just right. He smothers me with affection as if he's scared I'm going to up and leave any second.

I haven't told my parents or Lucas yet. Telling them will stir up old feelings, and while I know my parents will be happy that Deacon's on the scene—I'm not sure how Lucas will feel. Deacon was just like a part of the family before *that* day.

The day we never talk about.

Deacon's apartment is amazing. It's about four times the size of mine, easily, and has a view to die for. We look out over the Hauraki Gulf with a view of Rangitoto. It's beautiful and serene even though we're right in the city.

And it's like this place was just made for me with the window seat right by that beautiful view. It's perfect for me to curl up and read there while Deacon's dealing with a work issue. It's spring, and still a little chilly outside, but the sun streams in the window and all is right with my world.

My nose is buried in a book—which isn't surprising. I'm going through a romantasy binge right now. Maybe it's because I found my knight in shining armour.

"Pip."

I'm so engrossed in my book, I don't hear Deacon at first but squeal with laughter when he flops down on the window seat, stretching out and dropping his head on my lap.

"Have you finished work?"

He shrugs. "My guys are still working. A switch in the network failed, and I've had no explanation yet as to why the backup didn't kick in. So they're getting to the bottom of that, and I've come to pester you."

I chuckle. "You could never pester me. But you could wait until I've finished my book."

"Pippa. I'm dying."

Deacon's expression causes me to double take.

"What are you talking about?"

He looks at me with those puppy dog eyes. "My mouth needs your pussy, Pippa. I'll die if I don't taste it now."

I drop my book next to me and shake my head. "You're an idiot."

"I've been thinking about it all day. Don't make me suffer. Please put me out of my misery."

Rolling my eyes, I laugh. "I don't know if that's hot or you're sounding pathetic."

He leaps up to sit beside me and pulls me into his arms. "Whatever it takes to get you to come to bed."

"But I want to finish my book. I'm so close to the end."

Deacon shakes his head. "You always were such a bookworm."

I shrug. "I like to read."

"But you're seriously choosing your book over sex with me?"

Brushing my fingers down his face, I smile. "Maybe I could be persuaded …"

His furrowed brow straightens out, and he narrows his gaze at me. "Are you playing with me?"

"Not yet." My smile widens, and he tilts his head slightly.

"Such a tease."

He leaps off the couch and before I know it, he's plucked me up and into his arms. I let out a squeal, and he laughs. "You're all mine now."

"I don't think I've ever laughed as much in my life as I have with you."

His tender kiss makes me swoon.

"Just shows how compatible we really are."

He carries me into the bedroom before swinging me round and dumping me unceremoniously on the bed as I continue laughing.

"You have no finesse," I say. "You're no book hero."

His eyebrows rise. "We'll see about that. Race you to get naked."

I squeal and laugh, peeling my shirt over my head. This is one race I'm not about to lose. I've got no buttons, and he groans as his shirt slows him down.

But before Deacon sees me naked, I dive under the covers and pull them up to my neck.

He slows, his pants halfway down his legs. "That's not fair."

"Life isn't fair."

He chuckles, stripping his pants and boxers off and climbing into bed with me.

After rolling over top of me, he settles between my legs, his hard cock pressed against my thigh.

"So, what did you have planned?" I drape my arms over his shoulders.

"You, me, a lot of foreplay."

I laugh as he dives under the covers and gasp when his tongue hits my clit. I've never known a man to enjoy going down on me the way he does, and he's voracious with it.

I'm not complaining.

I'm also not complaining when he slides inside me, takes my hands, and raises them over my head, pinning me down while he kisses my lips and then my breasts. Deacon always knows just how to touch me and to make me feel wanted and needed.

Afterward, I lay in his arms and nuzzle his chest.

"What are you reading?" he asks.

I smile to myself. "That's a random question."

"What is it that you like about those books so much?"

I turn toward him. One of the things I love most about Deacon is that he takes an interest in everything I do. Doesn't matter how mismatched it might be with his interests, he's right there for mine.

"I travel the world without ever leaving home."

His lips twitch. "Do you want to travel?"

"Some day."

He plants a soft kiss on my shoulder. "Why haven't you already? I thought people your age were always going off to get their overseas experience."

"Did you?"

Deacon chuckles. "No, but I wasn't big on travelling. We formed the company while we were at uni, and by the time we graduated it was taking off. I just never looked back."

I suck my bottom lip. "I didn't have anyone to go with. And I didn't want to travel alone."

With a sigh, Deacon tugs me closer into his side. "One day we'll travel together."

"I like that idea."

He brushes his fingers down my cheek. "I'm planning on making all your dreams come true, Pip."

Gazing into those beautiful blue eyes, I sigh. "I've changed my mind."

His brows dip. "About what?"

"You're exactly what a book hero *should* be."

With a smile, he leans closer and presses a kiss to my lips. "I always want to be your hero."

As he drifts his hand down my body, I squirm.

"There's something else you should know," he murmurs.

"What's that?"
When his long fingers find their way to my clit, I suck in a breath.
"I really am addicted to your pussy," he says.
I roll my eyes and give his arm a gentle slap. "Stop."
Deacon's intense look sends a shiver down my spine. "I mean it."
His eyes search mine.
It's not the 'I love you' I want to hear, but I'll take it.

Chapter Fifteen

Pippa

By the time the night of the product release is here, I'm a bundle of nerves.

Everyone at work knows Deacon and I are together, but this is my first official outing in public as his girlfriend. While we might all go out for dinner or drinks occasionally, it's usually just the two of us.

I haven't made any friends outside of work in Auckland yet, but I have formed friendships with Simone and even Mallory, which surprised me. She's switched to being one of our most ardent supporters.

Deacon stands as I enter the living room, his eyes shining with happiness. I suck in a breath. I'm so in love with the gown we chose, and while it hugs me, it's still comfortable. Besides, I love the expression Deacon gets on his face when he looks at me in it. As if we'll never leave the apartment.

As for him—I've never seen him dressed up in a tux, and he fits it well. I let an audible sigh escape, and his lips curl into a cocky grin.

"Like what you see?" he asks.

"Yes." I'm breathless. This is what he does to me. I'll never get enough of this feeling.

"I've got something for you."

My eyebrows rise. "You've already done so much."

He shakes his head. "Come here."

I walk toward him slowly as he picks up a paper bag from the coffee table. My stomach flips when he reaches in and pulls out a long black box.

"Something Mallory said made me think that we should go all out tonight. So, I bought you this."

He hands me the box, and with trembling fingers, I lift the lid. Inside is a ruby pendant, the colour not as dark as my dress, but still, it makes me draw in a deep breath and gape at him. "Deacon, this is too much."

He shakes his head. "No, Pippa. It's still not enough to show you how much you mean to me." Reaching for the box, he pulls the pendant out and then motions for me to turn around.

I shiver as his hand brushes the nape of my neck, and I close my eyes—the woody scent of his aftershave surrounding me.

He fastens the pendant around my neck before placing a kiss on my collarbone and taking my hand to turn me back to face him.

"These too." He hands me a small box.

Inside are matching earrings, and I tear up. He's thought of everything. Infinity have several product releases every year, but with this being my first, Deacon's gone out of his way to make it special.

I love him so much that it hurts.

"Don't you dare cry," he murmurs. "Put your earrings in, and let's go. I want the world to see my girl."

It only takes a moment to switch out my earrings, and Deacon's affectionate gaze warms my heart.

"This is only the start, Pippa. I'm sure we've got years ahead of us where I get to be the luckiest man in the room with you on my arm."

I reach up to cup his cheek. "I'm the lucky one."

"I'm not going to fight you on this, but you're wrong."

Shaking my head, I turn away from him and pick up my clutch

purse. Deacon protested, but I managed to find one that matched my dress and paid for it myself before he could pounce.

I'm not stupid—Infinity has made him rich. But I've always paid my way and I'm not about to stop now.

He links his fingers with mine. "Come on, beautiful."

Every time he says something like that, my heart beats a little faster. I'm so in love with him, but I'm still a little scared to say it.

What if he doesn't say it back?

It's a smooth ride to the hotel where we're holding the event. Earlier today, I was here with Mallory and Simone as the conference room was set up.

There are tables around the outside of the dance floor, and a DJ who'll get things going after the formal announcements.

Thankfully, neither of us are any part of that. We just get to relax and hopefully enjoy.

That doesn't stop me from being just a tiny bit terrified of the whole thing.

Hand in hand, we walk into the room.

One look and I know this isn't my scene.

The room is full of beautiful people.

I knew there would be models—Simone told me as much. I've never dressed up the way I have tonight, but I still feel like a hobo compared to some of the women here.

Deacon grasps my elbow, and I lean into him.

"Nervous?" he asks.

"This is a bit much."

"You're my girl, and I'm showing you off." He brushes his lips on my temple. "Don't you forget that. I'll be by your side the whole night because there's nowhere else I'd rather be."

I love you.

I'm so close to saying it, but I bite it down instead and nod.

"Deacon."

I'm not intimidated at all.

That's the chant that goes on in my head as a blonde amazon

walks toward us. She's flawless, her face perfectly made up, leaving me self-conscious about my own efforts.

Her gaze is fixed firmly on Deacon, but his hand on my waist doesn't move an inch as she approaches.

It must take a lot of skill to completely ignore me—her eyes don't move from Deacon's face. But as if sensing my discomfort, his grip tightens and instead of greeting her, he buries his face in my neck and plants a kiss on my skin.

"Pippa, this is Adeline. She's the face of Infinity Drinks products."

I nod. I have seen her in the advertising before, but if anything, she's even more beautiful in real life.

Her eyelashes flutter as if she's fighting her distaste. That's all it takes for me to completely change my opinion. There's an inner ugly there that she's trying hard not to let surface.

"Nice to meet you." I smile as if my stomach isn't doing backflips.

"You too," she says before her eyes flick back to Deacon and a sly smile appears on her face. "Dance later?"

Deacon shakes his head. "All my dances are taken by this beautiful lady."

The smile disappears, and her eyes flash with anger before she turns and stalks away.

"That made me popular," I mutter.

"I don't care what she thinks." Deacon gives my hip a squeeze. "There's only one woman in this room whose opinion matters to me."

My heart warms and I lean my head against his.

He kisses my temple before grabbing my hand and pulling me behind him. "There's someone I want you to meet."

After leading me toward a tall, blond man in a tux, he lets go of me long enough to extend his hand. "Jacob Preston. It's good to see you, man."

Jacob grins. "Deacon. It's been a while. I don't even think you were at the last launch."

Deacon shakes his head, and I raise my gaze to meet Jacob's.

"Jacob, this is my girlfriend, Pippa Chapman."

His eyebrows rise. "Girlfriend? Someone actually tamed you?"

I laugh, and Deacon chuckles.

"Very much so. And I've never been so happy."

I lean on his shoulder at his words. I'm happier than I've ever been in my life with him, but we're usually so busy losing ourselves in each other that we don't talk about it.

"I'm happy for you." Jacob fixes his gaze on me. "What do you do, Pippa?"

I exchange an amused glance with Deacon. "I'm his PA."

He nods. "Nice."

"Pippa and I have known each other since we were children." Deacon tangles his fingers in mine. "She recently came back into my life."

Jacob shoots me a cocky grin. "And you ended up with this guy? What went wrong?"

I bark out a laugh. "Everything's worked out just fine."

"Well, you know, if you ever change your mind ... I'm available."

Deacon's grip on my waist tightens. "Never going to happen."

Turning my head, I kiss his cheek. "Settle down."

"You do have it bad." Jacob winks at me and chuckles.

"Stop flirting with my girl." Deacon's tone turns angry, and I'm not sure I like that.

"I'm sure she doesn't mind."

This went from being fun to serious in about two seconds. It's too much. I pinch Deacon's arm. "I need to go to the bathroom."

Deacon squeezes my hand. "Are you okay?"

"I'm fine."

His eyes search mine. "Don't tell me you're fine if you're not."

I lean in and brush a kiss over his lips. "I really am. I just need a minute."

He frowns. "Okay. I'll be waiting."

Nodding toward Jacob, I smile. "Good to meet you, Jacob."

I head toward the ladies. As the door closes, the loud sounds of the room behind me are muted, and I pause for a moment before heading into a cubicle.

I just need to catch my breath. This is all such a lot to deal with. I've never attended anything like this—the closest thing was my school ball, but this is the big time and a part of Deacon's life I'll have to adapt to if we're together.

The outer door squeaks as it opens, and the sound of heels clacking on the wooden floor tell me there's more than one person out there.

Taking one more deep breath, I stand and reach for the lock.

"Have you seen that woman hanging off Deacon? What's up with that?" One woman snickers, and the others laugh.

My throat tightens.

"I swore to myself this was going to be the year I bagged him," Adeline's voice echoes through the bathroom. "Instead he's got *her* hanging all over him."

My eyebrows rise. Deacon's wrapped himself around me to the point of suffocation tonight, and while I love it, it's been a little weird. And that moment with Jacob?

He's displaying to the world he's taken.

I grin. He's all mine.

My insecurities had flooded to the surface, but he's constantly showing me what I mean to him. I have to have faith in that. I have to have faith in *him*.

"I'll have to get rid of her. He's so much more my league than hers," Adeline says.

For a moment, I waver. Is this where it all falls apart? When all my fears come to pass? But Deacon wants me. He hasn't said he loves me yet, but he always leaves me thinking he's waiting for me to catch up while I'm already there. I've been there for years.

I should bite the bullet and tell him.

Flipping the lock, I take a deep breath and open the stall door.

Adeline's eyes widen as I step out and walk toward the basins to wash my hands.

She says nothing as I turn the water on and squirt the soap.

But when I turn to reach for the paper towels, she's in my face.

"I'm not sure who you are, but Deacon's on a whole other level to you. He'll ditch you anyway, so why slow things down."

One of her friends takes a step closer. "Addie, I'm not sure—"

"You're so not his type. I am."

I pause, licking my lips to give my mouth the moisture it so desperately needs. "Is that why he's never been with you?" I say.

She scowls.

My heart leaps. I didn't know for sure whether they'd been together at some point or not, but her reaction tells me I hit right on target.

I tug on the paper towels, pulling two out and wiping my hands dry before throwing them in the bin. "Maybe he's just good at seeing the ugly on the inside and staying away from it."

As I walk away, her friends part to let me through. Once I'm out the door, I stop and catch my breath. I'm not good with confrontation, but I will defend my relationship with Deacon.

I love him. He loves me.

I know he does.

"Pippa?"

Looking up, I meet Mallory's gaze. Her face is a mixture of curiosity and concern, but I smile to make her think I'm okay.

She flicks a gaze at the bathroom door. "Did something happen in there?"

I shake my head. "I'm fine."

Making a break for it before she can ask me more, I scan the room before my eyes find Deacon. He's in a conversation with Garrett and Victor, but he seems to sense my approach as his azure gaze hits me and tracks my steps.

He grins when I reach him, wrapping his arms around my waist and tugging me against his side.

"Young love." Victor laughs.

"Nothing better." Deacon plants a kiss on my lips. Out of the corner of my eye, I spy Adeline's posse making their way out of the bathroom and slide my arms around his neck. "Maybe we'll cut tonight short after all."

Victor reaches over and squeezes my bicep. "Seriously, Pippa, I'm so happy for you two. Deacon's always needed someone to keep him in line."

I drop my arms down to intersect with Deacon's and wrap them around his waist. "Tell me about it. He'd be lost without me."

Victor's chuckle makes me smile. "You know what? I really think he would."

He spots someone and waves. "We'll catch up again later."

Deacon nuzzles my ear. "I would be lost without you."

"I feel the same way."

He pulls back and meets my gaze. "You've changed my life. I don't think you know how much."

My stomach gurgles, and I laugh. "Sorry. Right when you're being sweet."

"I'm always sweet." Deacon pecks my lips. "I know I haven't fed you yet, so get over to the table and grab some food. If we're heading home early, maybe we'll stop for burgers on the way too."

I let go of him and place my hand on my chest. "You know the way to my heart."

As I turn to walk toward the table, Deacon gives me a gentle tap on the arse. "If only it was that easy."

But it is.

For all our fancy clothing, the food table is pretty basic. Mallory said they've tried different things over the years, but the most popular things to offer are things like pizza slices and sausage rolls.

It works for me.

And now my stomach's started grumbling, I could eat a horse.

After picking up a sausage roll, I take a bite. These things are small enough you can eat them in two, but if Deacon's promising burgers, I'll just eat enough to take the edge off.

I let out a sigh when I hear a woman's voice.

"The food looks good."

Right behind me is Adeline's group. To the left of me, I spot Garrett. He flashes a smile at me and holds up a pizza slice as if we're making a toast.

Adeline laughs. "The food always looks good. But I daren't touch any of it. No one wants chunky thighs."

They all cackle as if she's said the funniest thing ever, but I roll my eyes and turn back to the table before picking up another sausage roll and popping it in my mouth.

Deacon's with me, not her.

He wants me.

He must like me the way I am.

Mustn't he?

I hate self-doubt, but I can't help it as I keep my back to them.

"God damn it, I am *so* sick of those bitches." Mallory grasps my arm and leads me away. "Were they rude to you?"

I don't want to rock the boat, so I hesitate, and she clenches her jaw.

"It's nothing I haven't heard before. She thinks she's better than me because she's thin."

Mallory facepalms. "She's an idiot. You're gorgeous."

"I thought you didn't like me after warning me off Deacon."

She shakes her head. "I was wary. In all the time I've known Deacon, he's never been serious about anyone. At first, I worried he would hurt you, but the longer I've know you, the more I realise you're the one person who could really hurt him. But I see the way you look at him, and that's enough for me to know that won't happen."

I'm not sure what to say to that, so I hug her, and she laughs. "I do like you, Pippa. You're good for Deacon."

"He's good for me." I let her go and smile.

"Mallory, you'd better not be trying to steal my girl." Deacon swoops in and grabs me around the waist from behind, tugging me against him.

"Just take care of her, Deacon."

"Always."

Deacon nuzzles my cheek. "What's going on?"

Chapter Sixteen

Deacon

Pippa doesn't engage. She stays nestled in my arms, but she's quiet.

What the hell happened?

I take a deep breath in her hair.

"Did you just sniff me?" she asks.

"Guilty."

She laughs, but it's not a real Pippa laugh. It's half-hearted and it worries me. "What did they do?"

She says nothing, and I turn her around to face me. There's a smile on her lips that doesn't reach her eyes. "I'm fine, Deacon."

I shake my head. "No. Mallory said she thought something happened in the bathroom, and just then you two were deep in it, so I want to know."

Pippa shrugs. "Adeline was complaining that I'm in the way of her hooking up with you. She's not sure who I am, so she ... said some stuff."

"What kind of stuff?"

"That you'll dump me, so why delay the inevitable."

I grit my teeth. All this time I've known Adeline's been interested, but my image is very different to the real me. While I haven't had any serious relationships—not since before college—I'm also not big on anything casual. Hook-ups have been few and far between.

And I've never been interested in her. I didn't choose her as the model to represent our company, and she's just not a nice person.

The way she's treated Pippa? That's the last straw for me. I'll be talking to Garrett, Victor, and Mallory about moving on from her once we get this launch out of the way.

I grab Pippa's hand. "Come with me."

Her eyes widen, but she follows me, moving fast-paced to keep up with my long strides. We walk out of the conference room and into another, empty one where I close the doors. The muffled sounds from next door carry through, but here I can be alone with her, even for a moment.

With my hand still in hers, I turn and press her against the wall. Her eyes widen.

"Do you remember when I told you I was addicted to your pussy?"

She gulps and nods, uncertainty in her eyes.

It kills me it's there. I want her to know in no uncertain terms how much she means to me. "I'm addicted to *you*, Pippa. Obsessed with you. I don't know what you've done to me, but I want to drown in you."

She blinks rapidly.

"You're all I think about whether we're together or not. You occupy my thoughts. You occupy my dreams. You're in every single moment, and I am never, ever going to get enough."

"Deacon," she whispers.

"Don't you ever let anyone make you feel like you're not good enough. You are perfect, and I love you."

"You love me?"

"With everything that I am, sweetheart."

Her lower lip trembles. Pippa feels everything so deeply. I didn't want to tell her like this—I think I've loved her since I saw her again, but if Mallory's right, she'll have been hurt by whatever the bitch squad said in the bathroom. There's no reason for me to hold back anymore.

"I love you too," she whispers.

Pressing my forehead to hers, I take a deep breath. "Those women out there? They are *nothing* compared to you, Pippa. I wouldn't touch them with a six-foot barge pole."

She giggles, tilting her head up slightly. I press my lips to hers before deepening the kiss, savouring the taste of *her*.

When I let her come up for air, I brush my lips down her neck. "God, I just want to fuck you now."

"I'm not sure we're in the right place for that." Her breath tickles my skin.

"I'm not sure I care." I slide my hand up her thigh, up under her dress.

She gasps as I brush my fingers across to the waistband of her panties and slip my hand in.

"Deacon," she whispers.

"What did she say at the table?"

"Huh?" Her eyes are glazed over as I sweep my fingers over her clit.

"What did Adeline say to you?"

Pippa moans. "Does it matter?"

She's breathless. Just the way I want her.

"Tell me."

"She said she wouldn't touch the food because she didn't want chunky thighs."

Stroking her clit, I run my tongue up her neck. She lets out a sigh and rests her head against mine.

"I fucking love your thighs." With my free hand, I squeeze the fleshy part of her thigh to drive my point home. "Come for me, baby. I want to hear you."

Her breath is hot against my ear, and she's trying so hard to be quiet, but I don't care if anyone hears us. For the first time in my life, I'm in love and as far as I'm concerned, Pippa's my endgame.

"Deacon," she cries out, panting as I draw my fingers back out of her and over her clit.

She falls apart in my arms, shuddering as her legs go out from under her, and I catch her because I'll never let her fall.

When she straightens up, I keep hold of her while she steadies herself.

Not dropping my gaze, I raise my fingers to my lips and suck on them. "I need to get you home."

She looks at me from under her lashes. "I'm not going to argue."

Linking my hand in hers, I give it a squeeze. "Let's say goodbye to everyone and get out of here."

She beams, pressing a kiss to my shoulder.

Leading her out the door and back into the launch party, I cast my gaze around the room.

Garrett's on stage, and everyone's eyes are on him.

Except for Simone.

She marches toward us, one eyebrow arched high. "Where have you been?"

I grin. "Just gave Pippa a *come to Jesus* moment."

Pippa's eyes are wide, and Simone snorts. "I do *not* want to know what that means. Garrett's giving his speech, and he says you won't want to miss it."

A crowd is gathered around Garrett, and from what I can hear he's listing facts and figures for the year. He's a details man, who sometimes forgets not everyone else is.

"I'd also like to announce that ..." Garrett lets out a sigh. "This will be the last product release with our current face of Infinity Drinks, Adeline Walsh. In the new year, we'll be running a Face of Infinity competition to line up with our new health drink products aimed at a younger demographic."

To my left, there's a gasp and I don't need to look to know it's Adeline.

"Did you know about this?" Simone mutters.

"Nope. Garrett's making this up on the fly."

She snickers. "I never did like that woman."

Pippa's stiff as a board in my arms, and I press a kiss to the back of her neck.

"So, I'd like to thank Adeline for all the work she's done these past five years." Garrett nods toward her.

"This wasn't planned?" Pippa whispers.

I shake my head. "I knew nothing about it. Garrett has a habit of going rogue from time to time, but given he's the genius behind all this, we let him roll if it's not going to hit the rest of us."

"But why?"

I tilt my head. "If I had to guess, it's because she overstepped with you."

Pippa's brows knit in confusion. "Me?"

"Garrett knows what you mean to me, Pip. They all do. You're family as far as they're concerned."

Her expression softens. "I didn't know."

"Garrett and Victor and Mallory—they are my family. They know what I went through with my mum, and the four of us have been together through thick and thin. And now you're part of our family."

Pippa slides her arm around my waist. I wrap my arms around her shoulders and close my eyes, breathing her in.

Adeline's gaze is fixed on Pippa, and I glare at her until her eyes reach mine. She flinches before turning to one of her friends, and while I don't hear what she says, it's not good. But I couldn't care less. She had her claws out for my girl, and while I had no idea Garrett would do this, I'm not unhappy about it.

I've never been in love—never told a woman I love her. Not until Pippa.

She's it for me.

Chapter Seventeen

Deacon

After the product launch, we settled into a routine.

Pippa barely went back to her flat—it helped that she loved mine.

And it turned out declaring my love gave her even more confidence in *us*.

She knows she's loved, and not just by me. They know not to cross any lines, but Pippa's the most loved person in our team.

"You nearly ready to go home?" I ask.

With a roll of her eyes, she tilts her head, giving me an affectionate look. "Home?"

"Yeah. It might not be where you pay rent or where most of your things are, but it's where you sleep with me so it's home."

Her smile widens. "I like that idea."

"It could be permanent, you know. You could move in with me."

Pippa blinks rapidly. "You want me to move in?"

I reach for her hand. "I'd love you to move in."

"Can I think about it?"

Lacing my fingers with hers, I study her expression. She's always so open, but right now I can't read her. "Of course you can. Is there something stopping you saying yes?"

She bites her bottom lip. "No, it's just ... this is all happening so fast. I'm not complaining because I love you, but I'm not sure if I'm ready to move in."

Disappointment ripples through me, but I love her too much to push her. She just needs time and I need to keep on showing her how I feel.

"I spoke to Mum today. She asked if you were coming with me for Christmas."

For a moment, I'm dumbfounded. It's been twelve years since I've spent any time with Pippa's family. They know why.

"I'm not sure—"

Pippa's stern look brings a smile to my face. There's not a lot that can shake her happy-go-lucky mood, but clearly I've crossed a line.

"Deacon, Mum and Dad still think of you as their second son. You and Lucas grew up together. They'd love to see you whether you're with me or not."

Her brows knit, and I reach up and press my thumb in the gap between her eyes before she cracks and her beautiful smile emerges again.

"Stop it." She laughs.

"I hate seeing you so serious." I give her thigh a squeeze and take a deep breath. "I'll follow you anywhere, Pippa. Let your mum know I'd love to spend Christmas with your family."

She lets out a squeal before slamming her hand across her mouth. God, how I love this woman—so full of light and love.

I chuckle. "I'm happy that you're happy."

Her eyes sparkle with happiness. "You make me happy."

I wrap my arms around her and hold her tight. I'd do anything for Pippa—even face the man who helped wreck my life.

It's not going to be easy though.

"If you're not moving in, then move some more of your things over here. Make this place your home away from home?"

Pippa stretches out her legs. We got back to my place an hour ago, had a quick stir-fry dinner, and we're now snuggled up on the couch watching television.

It's like we're an old married couple already.

Married.

A thought starts to form in my brain about Christmas and presents for Pippa and it makes me smile.

"Could do, I guess," she says.

"So, I just realised that if your mother asked about me coming for Christmas, that means you told them about us." I hadn't pushed Pippa to tell her family—I knew she'd do it in her own time, but I was also aware she might not want to yet. Not with things the way they were between me and Lucas.

She turns her head toward me, her lower lip between her teeth. It's not fair she does that. I makes me want to suck that lower lip into my mouth and kiss the hell out of her, it's so cute.

"Did you not want me to do that?"

I shrug. "They're your family. Tell them what you want. Are you okay though? How did they take it?"

Her smile tells a story all of its own. "Mum and Dad are really happy. They were always sad they didn't hear from you, but they understood. Even Lucas was fine."

I swallow hard. "What did he say?"

"He just wants me to be happy." She licks her lips, and it's so distracting. "He also wasn't that surprised. Even back then he knew I had a crush on you. At one point he threatened to tell you about it, although he apologised for that a long time ago."

I frown. "When was that?"

"About the same time he got caught ... He was a mess back then. I think the whole thing with your mum really screwed him up along with everyone else."

Running my fingers through my hair, I lean back on the couch. "Can we change the subject? I'd rather not talk about *her*."

Pippa nods. "Sure. But you can't hide from it forever."

"Whatever happened to Roger?" I know at some point we'll end up talking out the whole thing with my mum, but right now I don't want to. Roger was always Pippa's cat. The Chapmans got him when she was five, and she's twenty-four now, so there's no way he's still with us.

Pippa's pained expression says everything. But I've gone there now and there's no going back.

"He got sick when I was fifteen. His kidneys were failing, and ..."

I take her hand in mine. "You don't have to tell me."

She shakes her head. "No, it's okay. I was there when it happened. He was put to sleep because they couldn't do anything, and he was miserable."

"He lived a good life. That cat adored you."

Tears well in her eyes. "There were times when he was my best friend. That year you left when Lucas was being an arse, I always had Roger."

I smile and squeeze her hand.

"I was inconsolable, and Mum and Dad put a ban on any pets because I was such a mess. But back then I wouldn't have wanted another animal. It was all too much."

Cupping the back of her head, I pull her closer. "One day, I'll make all your dreams come true, Pippa, and that includes having the house of your dreams and we'll get a cat. Hell, we'll get two cats. Whatever you want."

She laughs softly. "I love you."

I press a kiss to her forehead. If things hadn't turned to shit, Lucas and I would have been there to support and comfort her—the way we always did when Pippa was sad. But then again, our relationship now might not have happened.

There's no way to turn back the clock, and I used to think that maybe if I had that ability, I would have been able to change the way my family fell apart.

But now I'm glad because I'm in the best version of my life right now—with Pippa by my side.

Chapter Eighteen

Deacon

It's a long drive to Gisborne.

I would have preferred to fly, but Pippa's eyes lit up at the thought of our first road trip. How could I say no to her?

It's a six-hour drive, and I think she's just happy to have the reading time in the car while I drive.

I don't really mind. She takes a break after every chapter and looks out the window. So much of the scenery is paddocks and farms and so many cows—*so* many cows.

By the time we pull into Tauranga, she's finished the book she was reading and is onto the next one. I'm not sure how she does it without getting carsick.

"Exactly how big *is* this Christmas at home?" I ask.

Pippa leans against me. "We'll be staying with Mum and Dad. On Christmas Day, Lucas will be there." She pats my arm. "Gran and Gramps, Nan and Poppa."

"That's quite a crowd."

She takes a deep breath. "Auntie Cheryl and Uncle Pat probably too. Which means ..."

"No." I pull up at a red light and turn to look at my girlfriend, who's busy chewing her nails now. "Not Lizzy."

Pippa lets out a nervous laugh. Her cousin Lizzy spent one summer staying with them with only one goal on her mind—getting into my pants. When I think back, Pippa saw a lot of girls throwing themselves at me. And over the years, I caught more than one in front of her.

I reach for her knee and give it a squeeze. "You know I never hooked up with her, don't you?"

She nods. "I know."

"Did you ... keep track?"

When she shrugs and looks out the window, avoiding my gaze, I know the answer.

"I'm sorry, Pip."

She turns her head toward me. "There's nothing to be sorry *for*. You weren't to know what the future would bring."

The light turns green, and I watch the road, catching glimpses of her out of the corner of my eye. I can't turn back the clock—she was a child then, but I can make her a promise that she'll be the only woman I'm with for the rest of my life.

The diamond I bought her sits heavy in my pocket.

Time to turn the conversation to a lighter subject. We've still got a few hours left of the drive—we should have just flown, and I don't want to dwell on this for too much longer.

"That reminds me. I keep getting asked about this high-school reunion next year, and I keep saying no. Did you want to go?" I cross my fingers, hoping my girl feels the same way I do.

"Hell, no." She laughs.

"Really? I thought you'd be into that kind of thing."

Pippa laughs harder. "I hated school. It got in the way of my reading time."

I roll my eyes. "I should have known. You were a nerd." Nodding toward the book in her hand. "Scratch that. Still are."

"Hey." She bats my arm with the book, and I cry out, rubbing my arm as if I'm in pain.

"And I love my little nerd."

Her eyes light up, and the love she has for me shines. I don't know how I ever got so lucky as to be reunited with this amazing woman, but I'll always be thankful for it.

By the time we pull into her parents' driveway, she's nodded off to sleep, and I have to give her a gentle nudge.

Her eyes flicker open. "Are we here?" she mumbles.

"We are."

"Give me a second." She yawns and shakes her head as if trying to wake herself up.

"Take your time, sleeping beauty. But your mum just opened the front door and she's waiting."

Pippa's whole face lights up.

She opens the car door, and before I know it, she's sprinting toward her mother.

I laugh, shaking my head. She's not seen them in months, which is probably unlike her, but when she flings herself into her mother's arms, I get heart pangs. It's been so long since I felt like part of a family—and even then, it was part of her family, not my own.

I didn't realise how much I missed it. Not until right this very moment.

After getting out of the car, I take some tentative steps toward the house when Pippa's mother looks up and meets my gaze.

"Deacon." Her warmth washes over me, and for a second I hesitate. I knew coming back here would bring back all kinds of emotions, but I wasn't prepared for this.

Longing fills me. Yearning for that motherly relationship I never really had with the woman who gave birth to me. I thought I'd feel like a fish out of water, but instead I'm home.

"Mrs Miller," I choke out.

She walks toward me, and I stiffen as she wraps her arms around my chest. "It's so good to see you. Call me, Jean."

"It's good to see you too, Jean." I engulf her in a hug, and she kisses my cheek.

"Thank you for bringing my girl home. She's never been so happy," she whispers. "You did that."

"I love making her happy."

She steps back. "You were always such a good boy. Come inside. I baked a cake."

"Oh, that has my name on it." I grin.

"I baked two because I knew that's how you'd react." Her expression straightens. "Lucas is inside. I hope you're okay with that."

I nod. "It kinda goes with the territory."

Her brows knit. "I want you to feel at home, Deacon. We've all missed you."

Giving her forearm a squeeze, I take a step toward the house. "I've missed you too."

Pippa waits in the doorway, and I slide my hand into hers.

We walk into the house, her mother right behind us.

In the living room, her father rises from his seat, but I shake my head and hold out my free hand as I approach. He gives me a warm smile and takes my hand, enclosing his other one over it. "It's good to see you, son."

"It's good to see you too."

He drops my hand.

Pippa gives my forearm a squeeze and lets go, stepping away.

I see why when Lucas moves into the room.

"Deacon." Lucas holds out his hand to shake.

This feels like a test. I have to get past this for Pippa. I don't have to be friends with Lucas, but I can tolerate him for her sake.

"Lucas." I accept his handshake.

Pippa grasps my bicep, and I turn my head to meet her gaze. Tears well in her eyes, and while I still want to punch my former best friend, I'll keep it to myself because I love Pippa more.

"Thank you," she mouths.

I press a kiss to her forehead before turning back to Lucas.

"I ... I've thought about this moment for a long time. Back before you and Pippa were together. I can't apologise enough for what happened—"

"I'd rather not talk about it if that's okay."

He nods. "Sure. It's good to see you anyway. I'm glad you're with my sister. She's always loved you."

I wrap my arm around Pippa's shoulders. "It's good to see you too."

She slips her arms around my waist and gives it a squeeze. Making her happy makes everything else pale into insignificance.

"Would you two like a coffee? That drive must be wearing," Jean asks.

I grin. "I wanted to fly, but Pippa insisted on driving."

"I like the scenery." She pokes her tongue at me, and I resist the temptation to suck that tongue into my mouth and kiss her.

"Next time, we'll fly." I peck her on the lips instead.

She rolls her eyes. "Deal."

"It's not like you can't afford it," Lucas says.

I meet his gaze again and chuckle.

Pippa and I haven't talked about the business or wealth, but Infinity Drinks is a multi-million-dollar company and I'm a 25% shareholder.

Pippa's a hopeless romantic—it's all that time spent with her nose in a book. But I'm in a position to give her everything she ever dreamed of.

And I will.

Chapter Nineteen

Pippa

"Don't forget I'm going shopping with Lucas this morning," I say.

"Since when?" Deacon replies.

"Since we talked about it last night."

He laughs. "That was before you distracted me."

"You weren't that hard to distract."

Deacon wraps his arm around me and pulls me close. "Come here then, you little temptress, distract me some more."

I let out a sigh as if what he saying is unreasonable. The truth is, I love how much he loves me. He's forever reaching out and touching me as if he's scared I'll disappear. But the reverse is true too because I'm scared that I'll wake up one day and all of this will have been a dream.

"Kiss me like you'll miss me." I grin.

"Oh, I can do far more than that."

He slides his hand into my panties, and I bark out a laugh. "Do we really have time for this?"

Deacon pouts. "We can make time. We're on holiday."

His long fingers stroke my clit, and my breath hitches. I love him touching me.

Oh, screw it. Lucas can wait.

With a giggle, I pull the covers over both of us and lose myself in Deacon's love. This is my happiness.

It's how I want to spend the rest of my life.

———

Lucas glowers at me an hour later when I finally emerge from the bedroom.

"I thought we were going early this morning. The traffic will be insane. It's Christmas Eve."

I pop a kiss on his cheek as I sit at the kitchen table beside him. "But then you get to spend even more time with your baby sister while we sit in that traffic."

He fights it, but then he barks out a laugh. "Only you could come up with that."

"I can skip breakfast and we'll go now."

Mum plants her hands on her hips. "Are you sure you want to do that?"

"We'll grab something while we're out."

"Is Deacon okay with you coming with me?" Lucas asks.

I shift my gaze back to him. "He's fine. You're my brother. Let's go."

It's not a long drive into the city centre, but Lucas was right. The traffic is crazy and there are people everywhere.

Lucas grumbles from the driver's seat, but I ignore him in the excitement of being home.

It seems to take forever to find a park, and when we do, he grumbles again about it being so far from the shops we want to go to.

But I remind him that at least we're spending time together again.

"I don't need much. There are just a few small things I wanted to grab for tomorrow." I undo my seatbelt. "To be honest, I also wanted to spend a little time with you. But it's still hard, you know?"

Lucas nods. "I feel that Deacon's being polite, but that's about it. Not that I can blame him. I'd really like us to find a way back to being friends."

I bite my bottom lip. "I can't see that happening, Lucas. At least, not any time soon."

"Well, I'm here if he wants to talk. There are some things that he probably needs to know."

I frown. "Like what?"

"Things he needs to hear. I want to share with him first. No offence."

Swallowing hard, I nod and open the car door. I always knew there was more than what Lucas had told us, but he closed down after the immediate fallout and refused to talk about it.

It's not a topic I enjoy talking over with Deacon either.

We traipse from shop to shop and once I've found everything I need, I give Lucas the heads-up so we can go back to the car.

"Do you wanna grab some lunch?" he asks.

I pull out my phone and check the time. It's just before midday, and we've already been out longer than I planned to. But I don't get a lot of chances to spend time with my brother, and with things still awkward between him and Deacon, I'm not sure when the next opportunity will be. "That sounds great. Anywhere you feel like going?"

"There's a cafe just up the road that I like."

I wave my hand in the direction that he points to. "Lead on."

It's been a while since I've been home. Lucas went to uni and then came back to work for Dad's construction business.

We come to a little cafe that definitely wasn't here last time I was and go inside to order coffee and grab some food from the display.

"You and your ham and cheese croissants," Lucas says. "Does Deacon know you're addicted?"

I laugh. "I usually have one with my morning coffee, so yes."

We make our way to a table outside in the sunshine. It's a gorgeous day, and while I fully expect it'll start raining at some point tomorrow—it's almost a guarantee on Christmas day—it's nice to make the most of it.

It takes a few minutes for our coffee to be delivered, and then Lucas and I kick back.

"Are you and Deacon really happy?"

I can't hold back the grin that takes over my face. Lucas chuckles.

"I never expected this," I say. "When I turned up at that the job interview and found I was working for him, I was sure he would be hostile. But he's been wonderful from day one."

Lucas shrugs. "It's not like you ever did anything to him."

"Yeah, but I wasn't sure he saw it that way."

His face falls as he looks past me. "Shit."

"What?"

The chair beside me scrapes on the concrete as it's pulled back, and I turn my head to see who's joined us.

Deacon's mother's gaze is fixed on me.

Stay calm. She can't hurt you.

"Little Pippa Chapman. I hear you're in a relationship with my boy."

Is this woman for real?

She looks good—she always did. Her hair and makeup are immaculate, and while she's casually dressed in jeans and a pale pink T-shirt, she looks like she could have walked off a magazine cover.

Walking slightly behind her is a young man. It's hard to estimate his age, but he's easily younger than I am and my stomach quirks at the thought.

"We have nothing to say to you," Lucas says.

She pulls out a chair and sits. "This won't take long."

I shake my head. "I'm not having this conversation with you. Deacon's life is none of your business."

"It'll always be my business. He's my boy." She flicks a glance at Lucas, but she's barely acknowledged his existence.

"Who's made it clear he wants nothing to do with you." I lean back in my seat. "Now, I'm having lunch with my brother and you weren't invited."

It takes her a moment before she nods and stands. "Please tell Deacon I miss him. I'd like to see him before you leave town."

"Hell will probably freeze over first."

I don't drop my gaze, and after a beat she turns around and leaves.

Lucas grasps my forearm. "Who are you and what have you done with my sister?"

"I hate her." When I lift my shaking hands, he frowns. "I'm not telling Deacon anything about this. She can go jump."

"Hey." Lucas pulls me into his arms and hugs me. "It's okay. The wicked witch has gone."

"She can stay gone." I huff.

"Let's finish our lunch and I'll get you back to your man. Okay?"

I nod. I'm not about to let that woman darken my mood.

Chapter Twenty

Deacon

Christmas Day is a little overwhelming.

It's been a long time since I was part of any family, and the Chapmans are just so welcoming and wonderful there's a part of me that wants to run away and hide for a while.

"Everyone's coming for lunch, so we'll open the presents before we eat," Pippa says.

Lucas sighs loudly as we enter the living room. "Are you ready for the family onslaught, Deacon?"

"How bad can it be?" I ask, dropping onto the couch. Pippa sits beside me.

"The grandparents and our aunt and uncle will be fine. It's Lizzy you've always had to watch out for."

I pick up a cushion and throw it at him. He roars with laughter.

"I was reminded of that by Pippa."

He grins. "I bet. She had such a thing for you. It was a long time ago, but on the other hand—she's single again."

"I'm not."

"I don't think that's ever stopped her before." Pippa wraps herself around my waist.

"There's only one woman I want, Pippa, and that's you. And you know it." I pop a kiss on her head.

"Doesn't mean I'm not insanely jealous of other women." She pokes her tongue out.

"You don't need to be. But you do need to be careful, or I'll give you another use for that tongue."

The cushion hits me in the head after Lucas throws it back at me. "You can cut that out right now. That's my sister."

We all laugh, and it feels so good—like it used to be.

The door opens, and the living room is suddenly full of Pippa's family. She sticks with me, holding my hand and squeezing it as if she understands I'm a little overwhelmed.

And then before Lizzy walks in, Pippa gives me a gentle push and tells me to move down the couch until I'm on the end, anticipating her cousin's move.

Our parcels are already under the tree, but the pile grows as her grandparents settle in, and then her aunt and uncle arrive.

We never had Christmas like this back home.

Sure enough, Pippa called it. Lizzy walks in and takes one look at us cuddled up on the couch and rolls her eyes.

Lizzy's a good-looking woman. She's tall, blonde, and everything Pippa thought I wanted. It's probably why Pippa's a little paranoid about her. But I only have eyes for Pippa, and no one's going to distract me from her.

Her cousin's eyes dart to my end of the couch, and I swear you can see her mind ticking over as to what excuse she can use to try and make me move.

Pippa pats the spot on the other side of her. "Lizzy, there's plenty of room here."

With a huff, Lizzy makes her way to the opposite end of the couch.

"It's good to see you again, Deacon. You've made quite a big name for yourself," she says.

"Good to see you too, Lizzy."

She smiles, and I nestle in closer to Pippa.

"Why don't we get started?" Jean asks.

Lucas sits himself on the floor in front of the tree. "I'll hand out the parcels."

It only takes a minute, and the sound of tearing paper fills the room.

"Here you go, Pippa. There are two for you."

Lucas passes everything to Pippa, and she hands me my parcel.

"You first," I murmur.

She grins. "What's this?"

"Open it and see."

The bigger package gets opened first, and she shrieks when a new, top-of-the-line Kindle is revealed. She's been talking about how the battery in hers isn't lasting as long—although that's not surprising given how glued she is to it—and I went all out because she'll love it.

"Thank you." She flings her arms around my neck and kisses my cheek before returning to the Kindle box.

I nudge her knee with mine. "Open the other package."

This time, I watch her face for her reaction. I don't want to make her cry, but this might send her over the edge.

"Deacon." She gasps.

"What is it?" Lizzy asks.

"It's a first-edition copy of Jane Eyre."

I smile, and Pippa's gaze hits mine. She swallows hard.

"I love this book."

"I know. I do listen." I chuckle.

"I'm not sure what to say. This is the best present I've ever got."

I take her hand in mine and squeeze. "This is just the start, Pipsqueak."

"Don't call me that," she mutters, but the amusement in her voice tells me she's not offended.

She dives toward the tree and brings back a flat package.

"Here." Pippa's eyes shine with excitement when she hands me the parcel. "You'll probably think it's stupid after what you gave me."

"There's nothing you could give me that I'd think that about."

"Open it first." She grins.

I rip open the paper.

It's a photo of us from the launch party. I'd almost forgotten about the photographer we usually hire to capture the night. My throat tightens looking at it.

It's a candid shot of us. My arm's around Pippa's waist and we're looking at each other like there's no one else in the room. I know for me there was only her.

"Why did you think that I'd think this was stupid?" I ask.

"Because it's just a photo of us and not some crazy expensive present."

I gaze into her eyes before I place the photo on my lap and pull her closer to kiss her. "I don't need expensive presents. I just need you."

She snuggles in against me. "I thought you could put it on your desk at work."

After kissing her temple, I take another look. She's had it framed in a simple silver frame, and I already know where I'll put it. "It'll look great there. I get to look at you all day."

Pippa raises her face, and I give her another tender kiss.

"Hey, love birds," Lucas calls. "This is from me."

He walks over and places a long, flat gift on her lap.

"I don't know if you're planning on moving in together, but I'm sure it'll happen at some point. Anyway, I made this for your home—wherever that ends up being." Leaning over, he pecks Pippa on the cheek before retreating.

She picks it up. "It's heavy, whatever it is."

"Just open it, Pip." I laugh.

"You have to help me. It's for both of us."

I chuckle as I rip the end of the paper. "You do the rest."

She eagerly tears it apart before pulling out a beautiful wooden chopping board.

"Is that ... kauri?" I ask.

"It is. We had a job earlier in the year where the customer let us keep the offcuts. I was trying to work out what to give you for a Christmas present, and then you got serious with Deacon, so I thought I'd make you an early house-warming gift," Lucas says.

"It's beautiful. Thank you so much."

I slip an arm around Pippa's shoulders and pull her to me. It means a lot that Lucas was thinking of both of us, but is it enough?

I think what we're both putting off is the conversation we really need to have.

Chapter Twenty-One

Pippa

Deacon drops onto the couch next to me.

It's New Year's Eve, and we're here for two more days before returning to Auckland.

We've had a good break, but I think we're both ready to be alone together.

There's always a buzz in this place. Mum especially fusses over Deacon, and I get it—it's like her long, lost son has come home.

Tensions have even eased between Deacon and Lucas. I'm not sure they'll ever be good friends again, but they tolerate each other which I can handle.

"How do you feel about going for a walk?" Deacon asks.

He leans his head on my shoulder, and I rest my head on his. "I think I'd like that."

"We'll go visit our old haunts."

I laugh. "Are you sure you don't want to go for a walk with Lucas instead? I'm pretty sure you had more places to hang out with him than me."

He raises his head and places a kiss under my ear. "No, Pippa. Only you."

Standing, he holds out his hand, and I take it, letting him pull me up.

"Where are we going?" I ask.

"You'll see."

After walking out into the sunshine and down the driveway, we turn to the left and stroll the very short distance to the nearby reserve.

"What are we doing here?" I laugh.

"Well, I remember having to climb this tree to rescue a cat who probably didn't need rescuing because a little girl decided she would go after him and she got stuck."

I chuckle. "Oh, Roger."

"It's still the weirdest name for a cat."

I place my hand on the trunk. "You know, this is where I decided I was in love with you."

He grins. "And you were what, five?"

Nodding, I look up at the branches. "I was. You were the much more grown-up age of twelve. You and Lucas got me to jump and the two of you caught me."

When I shift my gaze back to him, he's down on one knee.

"What are you doing?" I whisper.

"Pippa Chapman. I have loved you for your whole life. Maybe it wasn't the same kind of love when I rescued Roger from the tree as it is now, but it was love nonetheless."

I laugh, covering my mouth with my hand. This is madness. I never thought that I'd ever find love with Deacon—not really. I'd always thought I'd watch from afar as he fell in love and married someone else.

"You loving me makes me the luckiest man in the world. Will you marry me?"

My heart races. I open my mouth, but nothing comes out.

"Pippa? You're scaring me."

Deacon never doubts himself, but in that moment, all I see is doubt reflected in his eyes. Does he think I'm not going to ... Oh wait ... my brain's saying yes, but my mouth ...

"Yes. Yes. I want to marry you very, very much."

He takes the ring out of the box, and I get a closer look. It's a simple white gold band with a large princess-cut diamond.

He slides the ring onto my finger as tears roll down my cheeks. I thought the best moment of my life was when he said he loved me, but this? This will never, ever be topped.

"It's so beautiful."

"*You're* so beautiful. I thought my princess deserved a princess." He rises to his feet. "I love you."

I sob as he gathers me in his arms. "I love you too."

He chuckles in my ear. "Can you say that with a little less crying?"

"I'm just so happy," I whisper.

"Me too, Pipsqueak. Me too."

"Don't call me that." I pull back and glare at him.

All he does is grin. "Stopped you crying." He places a gentle kiss on my lips. "Let's go tell your family."

"*Our* family."

Deacon's eyes mist over, and he nods. "Our family."

Lizzy's beat-up Toyota Corolla sits in the driveway, and I roll my eyes.

"Don't let that upset you," Deacon says, giving my hand a squeeze.

"I'm not. It's just funny how she suddenly starts visiting my parents when you're around."

He knocks his shoulder into mine. "Our news should bring it home to her."

I grin. I think I'm going to spend the rest of my life grinning with Deacon by my side. He's been so wonderful and accommodating coming back here for Christmas when he never wanted to return. But there was still a small part of me that believed our relationship was more one-sided than it actually is.

I've been in love with Deacon forever.

I know he loves me, but just how much I wasn't sure—still letting my insecurities beat what my heart tells me.

Every day he shows me that he loves me more than I realise. He gives and gives and expects nothing in return. Being with him is easy, and I can just be myself.

Mum and Dad are watching TV when we walk into the living room. Lucas sits on the couch with Lizzy alongside him.

Her eyes light up when we enter the room. I'm not stupid. It's not me she's excited to see.

Deacon slips his arm around my waist.

"We've got something to tell you all," I say.

Mum and Dad turn and smile. Lucas looks at us with one eyebrow raised. Lizzy fixes her gaze on me.

I hold out my hand, showing off my ring. "Deacon and I are engaged."

My mother cries out, leaping to her feet and rushing over to me. She wraps me in a tight hug. Dad's right behind her, shaking Deacon's hand before gently removing my mother's arms from me and wrapping his own around me.

"I'm so happy for you, love," he says. "Deacon checked with me a couple of days ago and me and your mum are over the moon."

I peck him on the cheek. "Thank you, Dad."

When he lets go of me, Lucas rises and makes his way over.

"Congratulations, Pip." Lucas kisses my cheek. He holds out his hand to Deacon.

I hold my breath, but only for a moment as Deacon accepts the handshake.

"I know my sister couldn't be in better hands," Lucas says.

Deacon nods. "I'll always take good care of her."

Lucas smiles. "I'm happy for you two.'"

"Congrats, Pippa." Lizzy waves at us from the couch. Her smile doesn't reach her eyes.

No. He's all mine. No amount of flirting is going to take him from me.

"Thanks, Lizzy." I flash my ring around a bit, making sure she sees it shine.

It's petty, but I can't believe she's still here to flirt with my fiancé. She can find her own man.

Deacon wraps his arms around my waist from behind, and I lean into him.

"I know what you're thinking," he murmurs. "No one holds a candle to you, Pip. I love you more than life itself."

I close my eyes as he plants a kiss on my neck.

Every day I feel more secure in his love—never more so than today.

But I still have that sinking feeling that something's coming.

Something that will blow everything apart.

Chapter Twenty-Two

Deacon

Getting back to Auckland has never felt so good.

I was wary about going back to Gisborne, even for a short time, but Pippa's family embraced me as one of their own and I got brownie points for asking her dad before I proposed.

I wait until we're at the door and Pippa's sliding her key into the lock before I wrap my arms around her from behind and press my cock against her arse.

"Oh, thank God we're home. I really need to fuck you."

Pippa laughs. "Can we at least get in the door properly?"

"Yes, but hurry up."

She pushes the door open, and we stumble into the living room together. After kicking the door closed behind me, I grab her hand and pull her onto the couch, on top of me.

Pippa laughs. "What *are* you doing?"

"Groping you." I run my hands along her spine until I reach her arse and give it a squeeze. "We're not staying with your parents for that long ever again."

Pippa rolls her eyes. "It's not like you got *no* sex, Deac."

I tug her closer into my side. "Maybe not, but I like it when you scream."

She slaps my chest before splaying her hand on my abs. "I still can't really believe we're engaged."

"Let's start planning our wedding. The sooner I tie you down, the better."

She snorts. "You can tie me down any time."

I knit my fingers in hers and roll toward her. "Now you tell me."

Laughing, Pippa squeezes my hand. "You always have a comeback."

"Everything's just so easy with you. I feel like I can really be myself."

Her expression softens.

It's true. I don't have to be Deacon, CTO of a multi-million-dollar company—don't have to worry about my image or letting anyone else down.

Being with Pippa has given me freedom I never thought I was missing.

"I'm so happy to hear that." She chews her bottom lip. "Thank you for being nice to Lucas. I can't imagine seeing him again was easy."

I brush my lips against her forehead. "No, but I'm not going to start trying to dictate your life to you and cut him out. He's your brother, regardless of what he did twelve years ago. You two are close. I know that."

"We weren't close for a long time after that."

I pull back and scan her expression. Her lips twitch, and she gives me a sad smile.

"I didn't know."

"It was his fault you left early, and you left for good. I was *so* angry at him. He was hurting, and he missed you. Everything was a mess."

Tucking a lock of hair behind her ear, I sigh. "It was a messy situation."

"I was a twelve-year-old girl with a crush. You leaving broke my heart."

"I'm sorry," I whisper. Gathering her into my arms, I close my eyes. Seeing her that last day haunted me a long time. I was so angry with everyone—so angry with the world. Pippa was twelve, and I was even angry at her for being there at the time Mum and Lucas were caught.

And then she appeared, and I knew she had to have walked to our place on that hot, dry summer day. I could have offered her a ride home, but I didn't—even though her presence that day softened my anger.

I have so many regrets when it comes to her.

I never want to let her down again.

"Uhh, Deacon?" she whispers.

"Yes?"

"I thought you were going to fuck me."

I cup the back of her head and kiss her hard. "You have such a dirty mouth, little Chapman."

Pippa sighs. "I can't help it. My fiancé's a bad influence."

"Well, get your knickers off and I'll fuck you."

She bursts out laughing. I love that sound.

Pippa rolls off me, reaches up under her skirt, and drops her panties on the floor.

"Now, get over here and sit on my face." I grin.

"Deacon." Her eyes are wide.

"Get over here."

She straddles my hips and slowly works her way up until she's positioned right over my mouth.

I grip her hips and pull her down, pushing her skirt back until she holds it in place. "I love you, Pippa Chapman."

She doesn't reply—she's too busy gasping and rolling her hips as I eat her pussy.

"Deacon. Oh my God," she finally cries out.

"Come on my face."

I suck hard on her clit, and she shudders, dropping her skirt so it covers us both.

Before I can say anything else, she moves down my body, unbuttoning my jeans and sliding the zip. I lift my hips to give her better access, and she pulls them to my ankles along with my boxers before scooting back up.

I let out a moan as she grips my cock.

"You're so hard."

"I can still smell your pussy on me, that's why."

She lowers herself onto me, and it's like coming home. It's not that we didn't fuck when we were at her parents' place, it was that we had to be quiet.

Now the sounds of wet, slapping sex fill the air as she rocks her hips, and I'm soaring.

"I need to see your tits," I hiss.

Pippa tugs her shirt over her head. I grab at her bra, pulling it down to expose her breasts and giving her nipples a squeeze.

"God. I could live in your pussy." I let out a groan.

She arches her back, but I pull her toward me to suckle on her breasts while she rides my cock.

"Deacon, I'm going to ..."

Her pussy clamps down on me as she rides out her orgasm, and I'm right along for the ride, spilling deep inside of her.

"I love you so fucking much, Pippa Chapman. I'm going to do that to you for the rest of your life."

She lets out a laugh and it reverberates through my body.

After tucking everything back in, she rolls to the side of me. I don't care that we're squeezed together on the couch. I've got my girl and that's all that matters.

"When do you want to get married?" she asks.

"Tomorrow."

Pippa laughs and slaps my chest. "Seriously."

"Tomorrow. Failing that—as soon as possible." I reach over and brush her chin with my fingertips, raising her gaze to meet mine. "I want you to be my wife, Pip. And then we'll find a home together where we can make babies and have the future you always dreamed of."

"We haven't even talked about kids," she whispers.

"I know. But it makes sense to me that you want them. It fits you, if that makes sense."

She gives me a tender kiss. "I do want them. And I want them with you. I want everything with you."

"We have that in common, soon-to-be-Mrs Miller."

Chapter Twenty-Three

Deacon

Pippa took to heart what I said about marrying quickly.

She pulled the wedding together in two months, and tomorrow, she'll be walking down the aisle where I'll be waiting for her.

"Never thought this would happen. Our last drinks with you as a free man." Garrett holds up his beer glass, and I clink mine against it.

I laugh. "It was just a matter of finding the right woman."

"I'm so happy for you, man." Victor punches my arm, and I nod.

"I've never been so happy. When we went into business and things took off, I thought that made me happy, but that was nothing compared to being with Pippa."

"You're a true romantic." Mallory deadpans.

"Ask Pippa. She'll tell you I am." I shoot her a wink.

There is nothing that could bring down my mood.

Tomorrow I'll marry the love of my life, and I'll give her the happy-ever-after she deserves.

"Can you do me a favour?" I ask Mallory.

She nods. "Anything."

"I know you're heading over to the Chapmans in the morning.

On the way, can you grab a flat white with one sugar and a ham and cheese croissant for Pippa?"

She's gives me the side-eye. "Sure. Why?"

"It's her thing. I just want to make the gesture, you know?"

Mallory smiles. "You're so sweet with her. I really hope you two have a wonderful day tomorrow."

"Me too. And with that, it's time for me to get some sleep." I stand.

"We should go back to your room for more drinks," Vic says.

I shake my head. "No more for me. I'm getting married in the morning."

I've been back in my hotel room for maybe five minutes when there's a tap on the door.

I roll my eyes. I'm going to get some sleep ready for tomorrow. If Garrett and Victor want to keep drinking, they can do it in their own rooms.

Tugging open the door, I speak before I look up to see who it is. "You two had better be ready in the—"

Mum.

"Deacon."

My jaw clenches. "Mother. What the fuck are you doing here?"

"I heard you were getting married tomorrow. Thought I'd pay my son a visit seeing as my invitation seems to have gone missing in the mail."

I snort. "As if I'd invite you after everything Dad went through."

She rolls her eyes. "Let me in. We need to talk."

Barging past me, she walks straight to the couch and sits down. I haven't seen this woman in twelve years, and she still thinks she can do whatever she wants.

"What do you want?"

"Pippa's not being honest with you."

I roll my eyes. "Is that really the best you've got?"

"Oh, sweetheart. Pippa knows I'm still seeing Lucas. She's known all along."

I close my eyes briefly and take a deep breath. "You're lying."

"She knew we were together that day. Lucas told her to keep watch."

Shaking my head, I grit my teeth. "She was a kid. You need to leave her alone."

"We had lunch together over Christmas."

Jesus. What the fuck is wrong with this woman?

This isn't the mother I grew up with. She's angry and twisted. I remember her being so angry at Dad leaving, especially when I made it clear I wouldn't be back.

He let her keep the house—in his mind it was tainted by her actions anyway. It was him who worked himself to the bone in the years that followed until his early death.

"Here." She hands me a photo. I roll my eyes before looking at it —only for my whole world to fall apart.

There's Pippa, sitting at lunch with her brother and my mother. Lucas is studying Pippa closely while her hands are up in the air— animated as if she's telling a story.

My stomach falls.

"Why are you showing me this?"

"Because you're my son, and you deserve better than to be lied to."

"That's a bit rich coming from you," I mumble. My jaw tics. Lucas and Pippa did go out together that day and came back later than expected. Why didn't she say anything?

I thought our relationship was worth more than this.

"I've made a lot of mistakes. But it's time for me to come clean. I'll go now. I doubt you want me hanging around."

Before I can say anything else, she gets up and walks out.

She's dropped her bomb and now she flits away without a care in the world.

This is twelve years ago all over again.

My chest tightens, and I feel like I'm thrown back in time.

Pippa knows how I felt back then—she knows how I feel now about my mother. Why would she hide this from me?

There's so much noise in my head and I can't get any of it to quieten down.

I need to get out of here.

There's no way I can leave tonight. I'm in no state to drive. But there is a private plane waiting to whisk us away on our honeymoon.

After picking up my mobile, I call the jet pilot. "Deacon Miller here. I want to know if we can change the time of the flight tomorrow."

There's a pause. "I can check. What time were you thinking?"

"10:00 a.m.?"

"I'll call you back."

When he calls a half hour later to confirm, I sink into the couch, whiskey in my hand, and smile.

To hell with the Chapman family.

God, it hurts so much to think that—they were nothing but welcoming over Christmas. But if Pippa knew, I'd put money on them all knowing.

Were they laughing behind my back?

No. They're good people. I'm sure if they kept it quiet, it was for Lucas's sake. They wouldn't want to rock the boat.

But it also means none of them were honest with me.

I was about to become a part of their family.

I'm not sure there's enough alcohol in this room to make me forget that.

Maybe if I empty the minibar ...

———

How long has that alarm been blaring at me?

I shake my head to wake myself up. My brain's on fire, and a quick glance at the minibar tells me I made short work of it last night.

Pain sears through my chest.

Pippa.

I push myself to my feet. Empty bottles litter the table, and I can smell the booze on myself.

Whoops.

Staggering to the wardrobe, I grab my suit and fold it into my bag. If it gets rumpled, I don't care. I'm out of here.

I don't bother checking out. It's 9:30 a.m. and I have a flight in half an hour.

Thankfully, there's a taxi right outside the hotel.

I'm sure I'll regret this later.

"Deacon?"

Mallory's voice comes from behind me. I swallow hard and turn. Confusion swamps her features, and her brows dip.

She's got the coffee I asked her to get in one hand and a brown paper bag in the other. "Where are you going?" She screws up her nose. "And why do you smell like you've been drinking all night?" She places the bag on a bench beside her.

"I'm out of here."

"What? Why?" She grabs my arm. "You're supposed to be getting married in an hour and a half."

"Pippa knows what she did."

I tug my arm away from her and slide into the back of the taxi.

"You'll regret this. She doesn't deserve what you're doing."

Shrugging it off, I lean forward. "Let's go."

As soon as we're on the road, my mobile rings, but I reject the call and shove the phone into my pocket. To hell with this.

To hell with everything.

Chapter Twenty-Four

Pippa

This is the life.

From the moment I got out of bed, I've been pampered.

My old high-school friend, Rachel, is a bridesmaid alongside Mallory and Simone. She stayed last night, so we spent the time reminiscing about our school years to Simone's entertainment. Mallory spent the night at the hotel with the others and she's due here any minute.

Mum comes in first. She wrings her hands together before Lucas joins her. Today's supposed to be a day of celebration and happiness?

Why do they look like someone's run over their cat?

"What's going on?" I ask in a shaky voice. My makeup's just been finished, and I loved the moment my wedding gown was draped over me. I'm surrounded by satin and lace, and I feel like a princess.

"I don't know how to say this." Mum's on the verge of tears.

"What is it? Is it Dad?"

Lucas steps toward me and drops to his knees in front of my chair. "Deacon's gone, Pip. We don't know where and we don't know why, but he's gone."

My head swims. "W ... what?"

"I don't think there's going to be a wedding today."

Pain and anger swells within me. Is my fairytale over?

"This is your fault," I hiss.

Lucas's mouth falls open with surprise as I brace my hands against his chest and push. He falls backward onto the carpet.

"Deacon has trust issues because of you. And now *everything* is ruined."

He holds up his palms. "That may be true, but he made a choice to leave. This is on him."

The door creaks as it opens, and I hold my breath before sighing as Mallory walks in. *Great.*

"Pippa. Are you okay?"

Hot tears spill down my cheeks. "Deacon left."

She nods. "I saw him get in a taxi. I tried to stop him and when that failed, I tried to call him, but he rejected my call."

I swipe away the tears with the palms of my hands. "You should be happy. You didn't want us together in the first place."

She shakes her head. "No. Not like this. He loves you. I don't know what's going through his head, but in the time I've known him, I've never seen him as happy as he's been with you." She crosses the room, and despite my pain, I let her take my hands in hers. Anger flares in her eyes. "I'll kill him when I find him."

"I just don't understand." I let out a sob. "What did I do?"

Mallory blinks back tears. "I doubt you did anything. Only last night, when we had drinks, he was telling us how much he loves you. He was so happy and excited about the wedding. We might all be friends, but I think he finally felt like he had a family again."

She pulls me into her arms, and I close my eyes.

"We were going to be a family. What happened to make him change his mind?"

"I don't know." She sighs, and I lean back to look at her. For a moment, she worries her bottom lip with her teeth. "All he said was that you'd know what you did."

Shaking my head, I wipe my tears away again. "I have no clue."

Her brows knit. "I'm so sorry, Pippa. There's no way I thought he would ever ..."

"I thought he loved me."

"He did." She sighs. "He does. That's why I really don't understand what's happened. He was angry when he left, and that's such a change from his mood last night. For what it's worth, he smelled like a brewery. It was like he'd been drinking all night."

Deacon's not a big drinker. We have evenings out and the odd drink at home, but neither one of us drink to that point.

What the hell happened last night?

I cradle my head in my hands. How could he do this? This man, who spent months telling me he loved me—telling me that he wanted to spend the rest of our lives together.

He made me feel like a queen.

What a hard fall it is to be dethroned.

"Pippa, your luggage is at the airport. I'll go and get it."

My head spins. "My luggage?"

"Deacon took the jet." Lucas squeezes my shoulder. "I'm so sorry."

"I guess he's enjoying our honeymoon on his own."

Deacon planned the whole honeymoon around everything I always wanted to see. Now he's swanned off to see the sights while I wallow in self-pity here.

When he left town the first time, I thought I was heartbroken.

But that's nothing compared to the pain I feel now.

Chapter Twenty-Five

Pippa

The first week is the hardest. There's no word from Deacon—no explanation as to why he took off. At first, I thought maybe he'd lied to me and this was some kind of revenge against Lucas. But nothing makes sense.

If that was the case, wouldn't he be crowing about it?

Mum is handling returning the gifts. I couldn't face it.

The first two days, I spent in bed before dragging myself out to breakfast on the third day.

"Morning, love." Mum hugs me. "Go take a seat and I'll bring you something to eat. Toast okay?"

"Toast would be great."

I take a seat next to Dad, and he reaches over, gripping my forearm. "How are you today, sweetheart?"

I shoot him a faint smile. "I'm okay, Dad. Just doing a lot of thinking."

He nods. "I guess you have some decisions to make."

"I'm going back to Auckland. My things are packed ready to move into Deacon's place, so I'll get them shipped into storage here and come home for a bit."

Dad frowns. "What about your job?"

I blow out a breath. I'll miss Infinity, but there's no way I can stay there now. I haven't spoken to any of Deacon's friends since the day after the wedding when they left, and they all insisted that I take my time making any big decisions.

But I'm spent. Even if I take the next month off, being in that building with Deacon doesn't have any appeal. Things will just be awkward, and I can't see how I have a future working there.

"I'm going to quit. If I hand in my notice now when I'm on leave, I won't have to go back to work before Deacon returns."

"You took the month off. It's not anything you have to hurry to do." Mum places the toast in front of me."

Movement from the door catches my gaze as Lucas slips into the room. His brow has been permanently furrowed since my aborted wedding day. I know he's concerned—they all are, but I have to handle this in my own way.

"I want to do it now and get it over with. The sooner I can get my things shipped down here and get out of my flat, the better. All I have to do is change the booking for the movers."

"But quitting your job? That's a big decision to make when you're so fragile."

Meeting her gaze, I shake my head. "Mum, I can't keep working there. Deacon's one of the owners. Even if I changed offices, it'd still be uncomfortable."

Lucas starts to say something, but I hold up my hand.

"I just want to go, get it done, and then come back here to lick my wounds a while."

"And then ...?" Lucas asks.

"Maybe I'll look for a job in Wellington. Or maybe I even start looking at Australia. I've got work experience. Maybe it's time to use my degree. I don't know."

He frowns. "I just wish—"

"Wishes aren't going to help me now."

He walks over and wraps his arms around my shoulders. "I love you, Pippa. And I'm sorry if I never told you that enough. When you hurt, I hurt."

"You're a good big brother. I'm not sure I ever told you that enough."

"Not good enough to protect you from this. I'm sure this has something to do with me."

I close my eyes and let out a long breath. "Maybe, but this was Deacon's decision. He could have left well enough alone and kept me out of it if that's the case. Instead he let me think—"

Lucas presses a kiss to my temple and drops into the seat next to mine. "He loved you. It was so obvious. He's not that good an actor. Something tipped him over the edge." He shakes his head. "I'm just as worried about him as I am about you."

I swallow hard. He's right. Nothing adds up. Mallory's take on the night before the wedding doesn't match with what happened. He either managed to hide his intention from not just me but his best friends, or he ... what? Had some kind of breakdown? It's hard to reconcile everything—especially with my own heartbreak getting in the way.

Is Deacon in trouble?

Now Lucas has sent my thoughts in a whole new direction and an uneasy feeling sits in my gut.

"Pippa. You need to take care of you now. I'll come with you to Auckland and help you sort out your things. We'll fly up and drive your car back down. Okay?"

Lucas lets me go, and I nod.

"Thank you."

He bops me on the nose with a smile. "That's my girl."

Chapter Twenty-Six

Deacon

I don't know why I came here.

The day I was supposed to marry Pippa, I put our travel plans in motion and landed in Paris first.

The hotel room was stifling, so I went to a club within walking distance. But no matter what I do, I can't stop thinking about my girl.

She's not my girl anymore.

My stomach churns at the thought of alcohol after my binge, and I must be the only person here not drinking anything other than cola.

A hand lands on my shoulder from behind and grips it, and I look up, blinking as I'm blinded by the flash of a camera.

What the fuck?

"Hi, Deacon. Fancy meeting you here."

I know that voice.

"What do you want, Adeline?"

She drops into the booth beside me.

"Oh, I've been reading *all* about it. You left your PA at the altar." She flicks a blonde lock over her shoulder. "I'm not really surprised, although it took you a while to come to your senses."

I set my jaw and glare. "What do you mean?"

Adeline places her hand on my forearm and smiles.

A chill runs down my spine.

"Someone like her would never be with someone like you. Not for long."

"Why would you think that?"

She throws back her head and laughs.

I assume it's supposed to be attractive. But I've seen the nasty side of this woman and it's true that when your inner ugly is exposed, it dampens the effect of the outer beauty.

"You must have been so bored with her. And clearly you didn't like her at the end—why else would you dump her that way?"

My stomach churns. Pippa lied to me—she kept something important from me that she knew would be devastating. But she didn't deserve what I did to her.

"You have no clue what you're talking about. Pippa's the most amazing woman I've ever met. I was never bored with her." My lips curl into a cruel smile. "You, on the other hand—I can imagine being bored with you because you're so one dimensional."

Her expression tightens.

"I don't even know why you're still throwing yourself at me. I've made it really clear I'm not interested. I did that well before Pippa came back into my life. What is your problem? Do you have no pride?"

She drops her hand, her expression stone now. All the laughter has gone from her eyes. "I thought—"

"No, you didn't think. You barrelled in here half-cocked and *thought* you knew how I felt. So, here's how I really feel. You are *nothing* compared to Pippa. She has more love in her than you will ever understand. She's smart and she's fun and she's a good person."

My stomach twists at my own words. I mean every single one.

I will love Pippa Chapman until my dying day—even if I can't be with her.

Even though I've broken her heart.

"And, Adeline. If you use that photo you just took to hurt her, I will end your career. Got me?"

Her eyes widen and she nods.

I'm not sure I could, but I can sure as shit do my best to make sure she gets no more work back home.

I take another drag of my drink and sigh.

What the hell am I doing?

I don't really know.

I'm still angry when I get back to the hotel, and I take my frustration out on the minibar.

In a week's time, we were scheduled to go to Italy. Pippa wanted to see the Colosseum and the Trevi Fountain. I'll take photos of them and maybe she'll think I'm doing fine.

The thought of her moving on without me makes me sick to my stomach, but I'm not sure how I can make things work after finding out she lied to me. Maybe she's better off with someone who's not as fucked up as I am.

Maybe Mallory was right when she said I wasn't good at relationships.

I'm not even sure what I'm doing here, but I'll press forward because the alternative is just too hard.

What a mess.

Chapter Twenty-Seven

Pippa

Rochelle hugs me when I hand her my resignation.

"Are you sure?" she asks.

"I need to go home and just mope for a while."

Her smile is faint. "I get it. I'm sure Garrett will give you a glowing reference."

I swallow hard. This job—working for this company—has been everything I wanted. It's not just about Deacon; it's about the friendships I've made here and the fact that I enjoyed the work.

But here I'm surrounded by memories that threaten to drown me.

"Thank you so much for everything. I'm sorry things have turned out this way."

"I told Deacon he'd better not do anything to mess this up." She sighs. "I wish he'd listened."

I shrug. "I don't know what's going on in his head right now. What he did has been devastating, but I can't help but worry too. I'm missing something."

She gives my forearm a squeeze. "Well, if you ever need anything and I can help, please let me know. I'll be giving him a piece of my mind when he shows up."

"I'm sure you will." That makes me smile. I knew she'd have my back.

"Just leave your swipe cards with reception on the way out. They'll get them to me."

Nodding, I turn to leave. "I will. Thanks, Rochelle."

I take a deep breath before I make my way to the elevator and up to the executive floor. It's been a long time since I've had the butterflies I do now—probably the day I interviewed.

After making my way down the corridor, I stop before the closed door. We were supposed to be gone for a month, so the offices had been closed with Deacon's teams temporarily reporting to Victor.

I swallow hard and slide my swipe card, unlocking the door. There's no point in closing it behind me—I won't be here long. Once I grab the few things I have in the office, I'll get out of here.

After walking to my desk—what used to be my desk—I place the small box I've brought with me on it and circle around it.

There are a couple of photos of Deacon and I, and I place them in the box before opening the drawer.

The second week Deacon and I were dating, he bought me a coffee mug. At the time, I thought it was cute. Now I'm not so sure.

It's plain white with black writing on it that says *Best Girlfriend Ever.*

Was that ever true? Did he ever think that?

Until I know why he left, there are so many unanswered questions in my head.

I place it in the box, along with the spare tampons and the odd bits of makeup.

"I was hoping I'd see you before you left."

Mallory walks in the door. Her smile is pained, and this whole thing must be awkward. Deacon's swanned off and left the deserted girlfriend to face the friends.

"I'm so sorry," Mallory says.

"It's not your fault."

With a shake of her head, she leans against the desk. "I know, but

I still think there's so much that we don't know. Something happened to Deacon. And it must have been something big for him to walk away from you."

Tears well in my eyes. "I don't know. Everyone keeps telling me how much he loved me, but the man I fell in love with wouldn't leave like that."

My phone buzzes, and I pull it out of my bag.

Frowning at the notification, I swipe up. Why would Adeline Walsh be tagging me on Instagram?

My throat tightens as I open the app.

She's in Paris—at least her location says she is. And there's a string of people tagged in the photos. The pictures themselves are from a club. She's dancing and drinking, and when I reach the last photo, I gasp.

Deacon's squinting—I assume because of the flash—but he's right there with Adeline's hand on his shoulder. She's beaming her million-watt smile at the camera.

"Pippa? What's wrong?" Mallory asks.

I slam my hand to my mouth, biting down on it to trying to stop the tears that threaten to fall.

She rounds the desk, her eyes full of concern as she pulls my phone from my hand.

The photo's still on the screen.

Concern turns to anger, and before I know it, she's throwing the phone on the office couch and wrapping her arms around me.

"I'm going to kill that bitch," she whispers. "Not sure if it'll be before or after I kill Deacon."

I bark out a laugh. "No need for extremes."

Mallory lets me go. "None of this is fair, Pippa. You did nothing to deserve this." She chews on her bottom lip. "I bet anything Deacon still didn't touch Adeline. He wasn't interested in her before you. Adeline was just too thick to realise that."

Shaking my head, I let out a snort. "She's not stupid. She's devious—I'll give her that." Sighing, I move away and turn to the window. "I know Deacon wasn't interested in her. He had plenty of time before me to be with her, and he wasn't. Plus, if he wanted to hurt me with this photo, he would have been the one to send it."

She grips my upper arms. "I'm glad you see it that way. I don't know what's going on in Deacon's head—he's not replying to any of our messages. But I have zero doubt he loves you. Something happened the night before the wedding. I'm convinced of it. I just don't know what."

I nod, and she rubs my arms. "When he comes back, I'll sit him down and talk to him. We'll get to the bottom of this."

Blinking back tears, I nod again. "I'm not sure that's enough."

Mallory sighs. "I'm sure it's not. He's a moron."

"Thank you for caring."

Garrett strolls into the room. His warm smile puts me at ease and without hesitation, he wraps his arms around me.

"Are you sure leaving is what you want?" he asks.

"I don't see how I can stay," I croak.

He places a kiss on the top of my head. "Any time you need a job, call me. If not here, I have contacts who would be lucky to have you working for them."

Mallory retrieves my phone from the couch before handing it to me. "Do yourself a favour and block her. She's stirring up trouble. We'll get to the bottom of this—I promise."

"The bottom of what?" Garrett flicks a confused look between Mallory and me.

"We'll talk later." Mallory pats him on the arm, and he gives her a tight nod.

"Thank you for everything. Both of you. I should get going."

"Do you need a hand carrying your things?" Lucas appears in the doorway, and I breathe a sigh of relief. I'd almost forgotten he was with me. Deacon's friends are one thing but having my brother here with me is everything.

"I'll be fine. I don't have much."

"I didn't realise you were here, Lucas." Mallory's smile lights up the room, and I meet Garrett's bemused gaze as she beams that smile right at my brother.

"Uh, yeah. I'm helping Pippa get her stuff moved home."

"We should go for a drink before you go." She shifts her gaze to me, and I swallow down a laugh.

I turn my head toward Lucas. He's fighting a smile.

"We're only here for a couple of nights, but that'd be great," Lucas says. "I'll call you?"

"I'll wait for your call."

Grinning, I pick up my box of belongings and make my way toward the door.

"Come on, Romeo," I murmur. "Let's get out of here."

He shoots me a side-eye before reaching for the box. "What? I like Mallory."

"Pretty sure she likes you too."

As we reach the elevator, I press the button and he turns toward me. "You think?"

"She just asked you out."

He scrunches his nose. "I thought that was an invitation for both of us."

The doors open and we step in. "She didn't ask me out for a drink before you arrived."

He's quiet on the way down, and once we reach the car, my mood falls. "There's a photo of Deacon on Instagram in Paris with another woman."

"What the hell?" He slides the box onto the back seat. Since he got here, he's commandeered my car. I don't have the heart to force the issue.

I climb into the passenger seat, and once he's seated, he grabs my hand and gives it a quick squeeze. "He's an idiot. But you already know my opinion on it."

"He didn't post it. She did. And she tagged me in it."

Lucas frowns. "That's plain weird."

"Is it? Or is it a message that he's ignoring me because he's with her?"

He lets out a sigh. "I don't know. If things weren't so messed up between us, I might have a better insight into Deacon's thoughts. But I don't. He never would have acted like this when we were younger—I was the flaky one."

After starting the car, he drives out into the traffic.

It's a quiet ride back to my flat. I resist the urge to keep looking at that picture for clues. I'm not sure what I'll think I'll find, but I'm after anything to put my mind at rest.

At least I know he's still alive and in one piece.

It might be small, but when we get home, Lucas carries my box of things into the living room before placing it on the coffee table. We're surrounded by boxes—all that's left is the furniture.

Tomorrow the moving company will come and pick up everything before taking it to storage in Gisborne.

"You should text Mallory and see if she wants to go for drinks with you tonight," I say.

"Tonight?" Lucas's brows knit. "You trying to get rid of me?"

I let out a sigh. "I need to go and get my things from Deacon's place."

Lucas reaches out and gives my shoulder a squeeze. "Are you sure you don't want company?"

Shaking my head, I use my other hand to pat his. "No, I'd prefer to do this alone."

"Pippa—"

"He broke my heart, Lucas, but I still love him. This is my last chance to say goodbye." I force a smile. "Text Mallory. If I can't get my love story, then I'll live vicariously through you two."

He chuckles. "You're still a hopeless romantic."

"Always. Go do it. Why are you hanging out with your baby sister and not the hot woman who's definitely interested in you?" This time, I don't have to force myself to smile. The idea of my brother at least getting his happy-ever-after fills my heart with joy.

His time with Elise messed him up. He also struggled with trust —just like Deacon. But Mallory's a good person, and I know she'd be good to him.

I'm not expecting him to skip off into the sunset with her but going out with her for drinks can't hurt. Besides, I do need to sort out Deacon's apartment by myself.

I don't want an audience for this.

———

After Lucas leaves in his Uber, I get in the car and make the drive to Deacon's place.

This is tough. A part of me wants to say to hell with my things and just leave them there as a reminder, but I'm not sure he'll care.

When I get there, I grab the moving boxes from the boot and carry them to the door. For the last time, I slide my key into the lock and take a deep breath before pushing the door open.

Deacon's apartment feels the same as it always did. It's warm and welcoming when its owner is cold and heartless.

This was more like my home than my own apartment.

I slide the keys off my keyring and drop them gently on the kitchen island. They make a *clink* as they land, and even that simple act leaves me feeling lost. After a moment's hesitation, I follow with my engagement ring. My finger feels bare the second it's off, but there's no point in leaving it on.

Running my fingers across the back of the couch, I take in every little thing I can. This place has so many memories—all of them good.

Why, Deacon?

Maybe coming here alone was a mistake. But I can't call Lucas now—he's at drinks with Mallory, and he deserves something good to happen to him.

I've only made it as far as the living room.

There isn't a huge amount of stuff for me to take. I have some things in the bathroom and the bedroom, and I brought a couple of boxes just in case I needed them.

But the thought of going into the bedroom makes my stomach twist.

I force myself toward the door.

The bedroom's quiet, the bed made and the room spick and span as it was the way we left it. Deacon teased me about making the bed with clean sheets before we left, but I told him that we'd be grateful when we got back.

Returning to the front door, I retrieve one of the boxes and go back to the bedroom. One by one, I open drawers, pulling out the clothing I've left here over the past few months. I'm so glad I hadn't made the final move in before the wedding. This is the last place I'd want to be spending hours packing up.

I press on, emptying out the bedside cabinet, pausing only to look at the photo on Deacon's side. It's another of the photos from the night of the product launch. Deacon's arms are around me, and I'm smiling so wide it makes my face ache even now.

He can keep it. He can come home and see my face beside his bed, and I hope it hurts.

When I'm done packing in the bedroom, I head into the bathroom. It doesn't take long to retrieve my things, and then I'm touring the rest of the apartment searching for anything else.

It's not fair. I loved this apartment so much. Sure, it's not my wedding-cake house with the white picket fence, but it's where we fell in love.

No. Where *I* fell in love. Lord only knows what Deacon was up to.

After packing the boxes in the car, I return for one last look before I lock the door and walk away.

I'm not leaving a note. He didn't have the decency to even leave a note for me when he left.

Now maybe the healing can begin.

Chapter Twenty-Eight

Pippa

One month later

After a week of me moping around my parents' place, I got sick of their prodding for me to get on with things and moved myself out to their beach house.

It's a couple of hours away from them, and I wanted space to try and recover from Deacon's cruelty.

I still have no idea why he left me.

I've called and left voicemails, begging for him to tell me why. But I think he's blocked me. He's ghosted me, and I don't understand.

Ten minutes ago, I sat on the toilet and peed on a stick. My period was due around the same time as my wedding, so I skipped it by taking pills, and then when it didn't arrive this week, I grabbed a test.

This isn't happening.

But the two lines show that it is.

My heart sinks. I've been sitting, staring at this stupid test ever since. If we'd been married, Deacon would have been happy. Sure, it's earlier than we planned, but our child would have been born into a loving home with parents who adored one another.

Now I'm not so sure.

Not when I've got so many questions about Deacon's behaviour.

Did he ever love me?

Nothing makes sense and this just adds to the confusion.

I force myself to stand and place the test beside the bathroom basin as I pull up my pants and take a deep breath.

It's late afternoon as I sink onto the couch. This is how I spend most evenings—in front of the television, thoughts swirling in my brain.

I turn my head at the crunch of tyres on gravel. It's probably Lucas. He's been there for me in a way he's never been before.

He grins as I open the door. His hand's poised to knock—despite it being a family home, he's also respected my privacy out there.

I fling my arms around his neck, and he hugs me tight, hushing in my ear as I burst into tears.

"Hey. What's going on?"

"I'm really glad to see you." I sniff.

He reaches for my hands and pries me away from his neck before searching my eyes. "Are you okay?"

"Just having a bad day."

Lucas pops a kiss on my nose. "Well, your favourite brother's here now, so that should improve it."

I snort out a laugh, and he smiles.

"How are you doing?"

I shrug. "I know I can't hide here forever, but I'm not ready to go anywhere."

He nods. "It's okay. You can stay here as long as you need to. I'll keep coming to see you if that's okay."

"At least I know you don't judge me." I move back to the couch, and he follows, taking a seat beside me.

Reaching over, he lays his hand on mine. "Never. I love you, sis."

"Love you too."

"Deacon's a dumbass."

I shake my head. "I just wish I knew ..."

He opens his mouth as if he's about to say something before closing it again and smiling. "It's his loss. I hope you know that."

We've had this conversation a million times, but it never makes me feel any better. Maybe it is his loss, but he's the one who threw me away. No matter how uplifting Lucas's words are, I'm brought down to earth by that fact.

I shrug again and sigh. "I just need time to process that."

He hesitates before leaning back. "You know he's due to arrive home today."

"Is he?" As if I don't know. As if the dates of my honeymoon weren't etched into my brain. Today was the day we were supposed to fly into the country. Will Deacon stick to that? Or will he continue partying his way through Europe?

Lucas arches an eyebrow. "Are you going to try and get in touch?"

Snorting again, I look away. "What's the point? I tried to call him after he left, but he's blocked me. You know, except for his Instagram account."

When I glance at Lucas, his jaw is set. "You know that's him trying to hurt you. I don't know why you look."

"Neither do I, but I can't help it." Tears prick my eyes. I've cried my heart out for this man, but there are always more tears.

"Pip, you've got to stop torturing yourself. He's an arsehole, and he never deserved you."

"I never did fit into his world."

Swallowing hard, I meet Lucas's eyes as confusion flashes across his features.

"What do you mean?"

I shift my gaze to the ceiling. "Deacon's life was full of beautiful, tall, thin women. Did he use me, Lucas? Did he make me fall in love with him just to dump me like this? Is this some kind of payback."

He grips my hand, and I fix my watery gaze on him.

"No way. He loved you. We all saw it. Hell, he even went

through Christmas with me because he was crazy about you, and he hates me."

"I just don't know what else to think." I clamp my lips together to stop myself from crying yet again.

"Well, I think being cooped up here for a month has given you nothing but time to dream up all these things."

His eyes are so full of sympathy, and I can't stand it. But he's here because he loves me.

"So, you're defending him now?" I'm being bullish, but I can't help it. My heart's been in turmoil since the day Deacon left and I'm no better than when this started.

Lucas shakes his head. "No, sweetheart. What he did was indefensible. I don't know what happened, but something set him off. Maybe it was being near me again after all these years. He hated me, and I don't blame him. He only tolerated me because of how much he loved you." He ruffles my hair.

"Hey." I laugh.

"That's better." He beams. "Anyway, I thought I might crash here tonight and go home tomorrow. We can spend the evening hanging out. Maybe watch some of that trashy reality TV you like."

"I'd like that."

Lucas pushes himself off the couch. "I'll be back in a minute. I've got a bag in the car—was hoping you were going to agree."

"It's not like I could stop you from staying."

He laughs. "I'm glad I'm here."

"Me too."

The one thing I'm grateful for is that this whole thing has brought Lucas and me closer. For the longest time I was angry at him driving Deacon away—I didn't speak to him for a year after Deacon and his father left town.

But he's been there for me this whole time. He's just on the other end of the phone when I need someone to listen to me, and he never judges me.

I still wish he'd never gone anywhere near Elise Miller, but there's no erasing the past.

The door clicks as he comes back in, and I pick up the remote. "Want anything in particular?"

"No, you pick. Do you want pizza? Does Tommy still deliver?"

I look over my shoulder at my brother disappearing into a bedroom. "He does. Number's on the fridge."

He flicks on the bathroom lights before closing the door. I keep scrolling through movies, pausing occasionally before moving on. I'm the worst at picking something when there's so much choice.

The bathroom door opens.

"Uhhh, Pip?"

"Yep?" I flick between channels.

"Is there something else you want to tell me?"

Shit.

I close my eyes. I'm so used to being alone that I didn't stop and think that someone else would be using the bathroom. Slowly, I turn, cringing as he waves around the white stick I peed on this afternoon.

Holding up my palms, I shrug. "Maybe?"

Chapter Twenty-Nine

Deacon

A soft hand curls around my wrist, and long, red-painted talons gently scrape against my skin.

"Want to come up to my room?"

The bottle blonde attached to the hand is pretty—I'll give her that. But she's all wrong. She's thin to the point of probably dangerous where Pippa is curvy. Her hair's not the right colour. And Pippa knows how to have fun without getting tanked on champagne.

Her lips, stained as red as her nails, curve into a sly smile.

"No thanks."

One perfect eyebrow lifts. "We could have a lot of fun."

As far as fucking Pippa out of my system goes, I can't. Even if I wanted to, I'm nowhere near ready for anyone else—even a meaningless fling.

"I'm not interested."

She drops her hand to my thigh and gives it a gentle squeeze. "I can't change your mind?"

Before Pippa, my dick would have stood to attention if a beautiful woman came onto me. Now, nothing happens. He doesn't even stir.

But if I go back to the room and picture Pippa's lush curves, I'll be hard in an instant.

It's not fair.

While I've been traveling, I also couldn't go to any of the places Pippa wanted to go—my heart just wasn't in it.

Instead, I've indulged and partied my way around Europe, telling myself I've moved on.

But I haven't.

Thoughts of Pippa consume me. When I'm not thinking about her, I'm dreaming about her. And every day it gets a little harder to think about the devastation I must have left in my wake.

All I have to do then is look at the photo of her and Lucas at lunch with my mother. It's enough to snap me out of it long enough to find a nightclub and drink to forget.

But I can't forget.

I should switch my phone off, but I can't do it. I've posted photos on Instagram all the way through my trip, pretending I'm enjoying myself.

The notification indicators show the calls and texts mounting up, but for the first time in my life I ignore them.

I need to work out how to live my life without the woman I'm desperately in love with. Nearly anything else in the world, I could have forgiven, but withholding the information she did and hanging out with my mother is unforgivable. She has no real idea of how much hurt and pain that woman caused, and the true toll it had on my father.

She doesn't know that the way my father actually died was by his own hand and not simply the stress and overwork he put himself through.

I made the choice to keep that from her because I thought that her soft heart couldn't take it. And despite me hating Lucas for what he'd done, I didn't want it getting back to him either. I'm sure he'd only feel responsible.

He's not the one I blame. My mother made a choice to throw

away twenty years of marriage by sleeping with a teenager. But the anger I felt all those years ago has resurfaced with Mum's revelation, and I'm clearly lashing out in the way I'm behaving.

I'm back on the plane tomorrow and home.

Home.

It won't feel like that without Pippa.

———

I'm numb by the time the plane lands in Auckland.

The wheels squeal as the plane skids into taxiing, and the rush of wind hits my ears as I both welcome and hate that I'm home.

Now to face the music.

I've spent the past month running from everything—the past, my mother, and Pippa. I can't keep running, and while avoiding my mother is easy, Pippa's a whole different story.

Whatever the reason, my friends will have judged me right along with everyone else.

I can't blame them.

Running the way I did was stupid—I know that. But the thought of confronting the situation is still so raw. All I've done is delay things.

Shame floods my system. At some point, I'll reach out to Pippa. There's no excuse for what she did, but I could have handled it better.

Every time I pictured her in her wedding dress, waiting for me, I had a drink. There wasn't enough alcohol in Europe to absolve me of that.

Once I'm through customs, I head outside the terminal and jump in a taxi.

I can't wait to get home and sleep in my own bed.

There won't be much of Pippa left at home. Even if she hasn't cleared out her things, there wasn't a lot to start with. She'd started the process of moving, but the majority of her things were yet to be shifted.

It's a depressing thought.

I don't stop when I walk in the door and lock it behind me. Leaving my bags in the living room, I head straight for my bed and collapse onto it.

After the past month, I could sleep for a week.

My gaze falls on the photo beside the bed.

Pippa in that red dress, her neck glittering with the ruby I bought her to match, my arms wrapped around her waist—the way it was nearly the whole night.

That's the night I told her I loved her for the first time.

I turn my head rather than look at it. The pain grows again—every time I beat it down, it reappears.

I grab her pillow and pull it toward me, breathing in the scent of her.

What the fuck do I do now?

Chapter Thirty

Deacon

For the past four weeks, I've not spoken to anyone back home.

My phone is overflowing with missed calls and voicemails, but I've buried my head in the sand—always putting off dealing with this until I came back.

Maybe I'll just buy a new phone.

I wait until the meeting's started. When I arrived this morning, I kept my head down, not meeting anyone's gaze.

I've got no one to blame but myself.

Inside I'm a mess, but that's the last thing I want to show anyone.

So, I'll hold my head up high and make out I'm proud of everything I've done—all the while, dying inside.

Back when my parents split, I saw a therapist for a while. She helped me with my anger over everything, and I thought I'd been able to move on. I haven't.

It's time to find a new therapist and get help. There's no point going after Pippa—she'll never forgive me for the way I've treated her. It's better she move on and find someone who isn't so messed up.

The thought of that rips me apart, but I can't see how this ends any other way.

When I get to the boardroom, I pause before reaching for the door handle. Time to pull myself together and bullshit my way through this.

Every head turns when I push open the door, and I take a deep breath and smile.

"Morning everyone."

I drop into a nearby chair, forcing my smile to continue as the other three look at me.

"Oh, by the way, Garrett. You're welcome to have Pippa as your PA. Obviously she can't work for me anymore."

Mallory snorts, and I shift my gaze to her before Garrett speaks up.

"Pippa's welcome to work with me any time. She's probably the best PA the company's ever seen."

"Well, she is *all yours.*" I lean back in my chair. "What else has been happening while I've been away."

"You're an arsehole." Mallory crosses her arms.

"Pippa quit. Did you expect her to do anything different?" Victor asks. "I don't know what's going on with you, but she was a mess after you ditched her at the wedding."

My chest tightens. The thought of how Pippa must have felt that day has haunted me this past month. But she made her choice when she hid the truth from me.

"Pippa wasn't the woman I thought she was."

"In what way?" Victor leans forward in his chair. "You two were in love one minute, and the next thing you're running away."

"I don't know what to say to you. You weren't there to see how devastated she was." Mallory shakes her head. "I'm not sure who you are anymore."

"Then maybe you never really knew me."

Her eyes well with tears. "I'm beginning to realise that."

"Deacon. Talk to us. We're all here for you. Something went down between when you had drinks with us and you leaving. Maybe we can help." There's a softness to Garrett's voice that's not usually there. I know he cares—they all do.

Maybe I don't deserve any sympathy. Pippa's the one who needs the support.

I'm not surprised she's quit. If I were in her shoes, I'd quit too. I hate that she feels she can't work here anymore, but I also can't blame her.

I did this.

I hate myself for it.

———

Pippa's desk is spotless.

I'm not sure I expected anything else, but it still hits me hard.

I run my finger along the edge. God how I wish I could rewind to just a few weeks ago when I was oblivious to my mother and Lucas. Pippa and I were so happy.

No matter what I try and tell myself, it's been her on my mind every second the whole month I was gone.

She's all I ever wanted.

"So, you're back." Rochelle's voice comes from the door.

I turn. She stalks toward me but comes to a halt on the other side of the desk.

"Pippa resigned," she says, crossing her arms. "I've got no idea what is going through your head, but you swore to me that you wouldn't hurt her. You're damn lucky she's not involving the company in this."

I shrug. "Things just didn't work out."

"What the hell, Deacon?"

I've never heard Rochelle this upset. The tearful tone in her voice rips another hole straight through me. First Mallory, now Rochelle. Looks like I'm breaking hearts everywhere.

"She hid something important from me—something that if she'd just been honest about, I wouldn't be so angry."

"And it was enough to jilt her on her wedding day?"

I look away. What I did was heartless and done on the spur of the moment. I can regret how I did it without regretting why.

Meeting her gaze, I condemn myself. "What's done is done."

Her brows dip, and she glares at me. I turn back toward the window under her heavy gaze, and I stare at nothing but the sky until the office door slams behind me.

What am I doing?

I'm as much in love with Pippa as I was before my mother dropped her bombshell.

There's no way back to where we were. I've fucked up everything.

The worst part of all this is that I've known this for the entire month I've been away.

I've just been too afraid to face it.

Chapter Thirty-One

Deacon

My apartment feels empty.

I'm not sure it'll ever be brought back to life the way it was when Pippa was here.

Yesterday when I got in, I went straight to the bedroom to crash. Pippa's scent was still in her pillow, and it tickled my nose when I grabbed it to sleep.

She freshly made the bed before we left, and I regret that to my core.

I'm a goddam mess.

Heading into the kitchen, I come to a halt when I reach the island.

The glint of metal hits me, and I struggle to breathe.

She's been here.

Her engagement ring, and her house key sit in the centre of the island. Pippa might not have left me a note, but she left me a message.

What the hell did I do?

After pouring myself a scotch, I set it down on the coffee table and take a seat on the couch before loosening my tie.

She might be gone from my life, but everything and everywhere reminds me of her.

It's my own fault. I let her under my skin when I should have known better than to trust her.

There's a loud rap at my door.

"Holy shit." My hand flies to my chest as the silence of my apartment is shattered. "Who is it?" I yell.

"Deacon, it's Lucas. I need to talk to you."

I drain my drink and stand, taking in a long, deep breath before huffing it out and walking toward the door. "What do you want?"

"Let me in. I have to talk to you about Pippa."

I tug the door open. His gaze, so much like his sister's, hits me and I draw in a sharp breath. "Pippa's not my concern anymore."

"I disagree." He lodges his body in the doorway as I try and close the door again.

"I'm not interested in anything you have to say." I set my jaw and glare at him.

"Tough shit. I'm not leaving until I'm done."

He pushes past me, and I grit my teeth before pushing the door shut and turning toward him. "There's nothing you can say that will change anything."

Lucas chuckles. "You look as bad as Pippa does. I'm glad to see that. If you didn't, I'd think you didn't still love her."

I clamp my jaw together.

"Deacon, I know you love her. And I don't know why you left, but there are some things I want to tell you as I'm trying to make sense of all of this."

Running my tongue across my teeth, I pause before responding. "It's done, Lucas. Pippa and I are over."

He shakes his head. "No, you're not."

I turn my back on him. "You can leave now."

Silence falls heavy on us. And I drop myself onto the couch once more.

He mimics the movement, taking a seat beside me. "Your mother groomed me. I was twelve when it started."

My throat tightens. "What?" The word comes out in a croak and for a moment my head feels light, like I'm about to faint.

"It started with little comments. How mature I was. How I seemed older than other boys my age." He knits his fingers together and shifts his gaze to meet mine. "Then the touching started. Nothing too obvious, but a brush of her hand on my arm at first. Over time, she grew more confident and, dude, your mum was hot."

I drop my gaze.

"By the time she slid her hand into my pants, I was fifteen and ready to go. But she told me she didn't want to cross too many lines until I was sixteen. I was staying the night at your place and went downstairs for a drink. She gave me a blow job. I thought I was in heaven." He lets out a hollow laugh. "A year later, we had sex. I really did think I was such a big man because she told me I was, when really I'd been abused."

He falls silent.

I scrape my nails over my palms. "So, why did you keep sleeping with her?"

"The last time was when you caught us. After it all sunk in, I can't even begin to describe how much shame I felt. It was like everything hit home at once."

Shaking my head, I meet his eyes. "No. She told me you were still sleeping together."

"When?" His brows knit, and a sick sensation rolls over my stomach.

"The night before the wedding."

He narrows his eyes. "She came to see you the night before the wedding? I thought it was made clear to her that she was to stay away."

I shrug. "I thought so, but she insisted. She told me you'd been sleeping together all this time and that Pippa knew all about it." Huffing out a breath, I glance down at my fisted hands and then back at him. "Lucas, I loved your sister so much, but to find out the secret she kept from me—something she knew would hurt me."

Lucas runs his hand through his dark hair. "You really believed your mother? After everything she did to hurt you and your father?"

"Well, I—"

Reality hits me like a ton of bricks.

Mum did what she does best—she lied to me.

I believed every word she said.

"There were photos of the three of you having a cosy little lunch."

Lucas's eyebrows arch. "Ha." He nods.

"So you don't deny it?"

He pins his bottom lip with his teeth while eyeing me up. "I had lunch with my little sister while you two were home for Christmas. Remember that?"

I nod slowly. "She said she had some Christmas shopping to do."

"Yeah, she did. She had a couple of gifts she wanted to get you, and afterward we went to a cafe for lunch. Your mother turned up, uninvited, and sat at our table."

My stomach sinks.

"She said she'd heard you and Pippa were serious, and she tried to stick her nose into your business. Pippa told her where to go."

Shit.

I wince.

"What's funny is Elise didn't even look at me. She turned your whole world upside down and barely acknowledged my presence. And it seemed to me like she had a new man, or rather boy, to run around after her." He huffs out a breath. "I don't know how there were photos—maybe he took them—but we didn't ask her to join us."

He raises his right hand and stabs me in the chest with his index finger.

"You broke her, Deacon. She's been a mess ever since you left. You must know she quit her job and moved into Mum and Dad's beach house."

I shake my head. "I knew she'd quit."

"I'm not sure she'll ever be the same again. She won't talk about it other than asking if she wasn't good enough, and she's not taking care of herself—not in the way she should be. Mum and Dad are so worried about her, but she won't see a therapist."

I did that.

My beautiful Pippa. My carefree, always smiling Pippa.

"I'm such an arsehole." I let out a groan.

Lucas holds up his palms. "You'll get no argument from me."

"I was so angry." I swallow, but there's a lump in my throat and all I can taste is bile. "Oh, God, Lucas. What the hell did I do?"

"She was humiliated and heartbroken. And those Instagram photos?"

Fuck.

"She saw them all. I'm *so* worried about her."

My head spins. I grip the arm of the couch, unable to meet Lucas's gaze. I'm such a fool. I knew Mum was angry that Dad left and I chose to follow him. But I was old enough to make up my own mind and not want anything to do with her.

Why the hell did I fall so easily into her trap?

Pippa never gave me any reason to doubt her. I let my mother get in my head and broke my beautiful girl's heart.

"I could have come in here and laid you out. God knows I've wanted to punch you repeatedly this past month. But Pippa's far more important to me than risking an assault charge, and I needed you to know the full story."

My whole body shudders. I swore I'd never hurt her, and that's exactly what I did. For no reason. When I should have gone to talk to her—confronted her with what I had—I ran instead.

"How ... how do I fix this?"

He shrugs. "I'm not sure you can. If you're going to fuck with her again, you need to stay away and give her time to heal. You know she's been in love with you since she was a kid, right?"

Numbness spreads up my neck, but I nod.

"Those damn photos. There's not been anyone else. I just made it look like that because I wanted to hurt her the way I was hurting. What the hell is wrong with me?"

"The only person who can answer that is you." He sets his jaw. "I'm going to talk to the police about your mother. Who knows if anything can be done, but if she did that to me then she's capable of doing it to someone else. And her new man does look awfully young."

My stomach rolls. "I had no idea."

"No one does. I haven't told Pippa or my parents."

I meet his hazel-eyed gaze—the one he shares with Pippa. "You kept this to yourself?"

"It was easier for people to be angry with me than admit I was groomed. And hell, by the time I saw it for what it was, it was humiliating. Pippa's not the only one who needs therapy."

Burying my face in my hands, I let out a sigh as he grips my shoulder.

"I won't lie. You've got a long road ahead of you if you want to regain her trust."

My head's still spinning, but there's only one thing I want out of this influx of information.

"What do I do, Lucas? She told me how much she hurt when I left town the first time—now I've done this, how can we ever get back to what we had?"

He tilts his head. "Patience and time. You know what Pippa's like. She's all heart. And right now, that heart is shattered. At least she's talking to me this time."

I frown. "What do you mean?"

Huffing out a breath, he drops his gaze. "She didn't speak to me for a year after you and your father left."

Despite my agony, I bark out a laugh. "Really? I didn't know that."

"I always thought it was such a pain in the arse having a little sister, but I'd have done anything to hear her voice back then." He nudges my knee with his. "I know she tried to reach you. Did you block her?"

I shake my head. "Thought about it. Couldn't do it. She left me voicemails, but I was so angry that I didn't listen to them."

"Maybe start there. You need to understand the devastation you left in your wake before you can move forward." He stands. "I'm flying back home again tonight, but I'll leave you my number in case you want to call after you've listened."

I nod.

"She loves you, Deacon. I wouldn't be here if she didn't. So, I need you to either man up and try and sort things out or just leave her alone. She doesn't need the torment she's going through now."

In the quiet of my apartment, I stare at my phone screen. Lucas is right. I need to listen to her. It's the least I deserve.

I dial into my voicemail and close my eyes.

I'm not even three messages in and I'm a mess. She's distraught—I've never heard her so desperate.

And she's blaming herself.

She didn't even know why I'd left, and she blamed herself. I thought our time together had built her up—her confidence had grown so much. But in the act of leaving, I undid all the work she'd put into herself.

It's so hard to hear, but I press on. The pain and desperation in her voice give way to her pleading with me to let her know I'm okay.

By the time I'm finished, I'm empty—my heart is aching and all I want is to hold her in my arms.

There's a long road ahead of me if I beg her for forgiveness.

But Pippa's worth every single bit of it.

Chapter Thirty-Two

Pippa

When I was younger, we spent our summers between home and our holiday house. I thought that the beach would have some magical healing properties—it always made me feel better as a child. But it's been a month and that's evidently not the case.

How do I move on?

I was going to marry the man of my dreams—the man I'd loved my whole life. And now? Now I don't know how to keep going.

I'm sure everyone thinks I'm a fool to still be this heartbroken when Deacon's made it clear he's getting on with his life. And I'm not doing myself any good stalking his Instagram, seeing he's out there with other women—living his life while I sit here day after day not knowing what to do next.

The only thing I do know is that I have to go on, and I have to find a way to make a new life without him. I need to look after myself and the baby I'm carrying. Hell, I need to drag myself to the doctor's office for a check-up, but I haven't managed to do that yet.

The first thing I do in the morning is check Deacon's Instagram. I shouldn't—all it does is dig the pain in deeper.

What the hell?

Every photo he's taken in the past month is gone.

The last photo he has still up is the one he posted for our engagement. He's smiling at the camera. I'm smiling at him like he hung the moon. He did. He still does.

What does this mean?

It'd be far too easy to read something into this. Maybe Garrett, Victor, and Mallory told him it made the company look bad—I don't know. He surely hasn't had a change of heart.

I'm not sure I'd know what to do if he did.

Even if we're never together, I still want some answers.

Why did he leave?

Why did he make things worse every day posting those images?

How could he spend time with Adeline after she disrespected me?

Thinking about this whole thing sends me spiralling again. It's the hell I've lived in this past month, unable to move forward.

I know I have to eventually, but until then I'm going to second guess everything in my life.

By early afternoon, the constant buzzing in my head has become unbearable, and I give up trying to read and head out to the beach.

Sitting on the sand with the sea breeze flowing doesn't completely clear my mind, but it gives me a break from the heavy stuff.

I draw in a deep breath of sea air and cross my fingers with a quick prayer that it'll help me sleep better tonight.

I'm sure it won't, but I can have hope.

"Penny for your thoughts."

I'm hearing things. *I must be.*

Deacon's back at work. He's definitely not here with me on this beach.

I thought he loved me, but it's clear it was all just some game to him.

"Pipsqueak."

Something brushes my hand, and I look down to find a man's fingers lingering on my skin.

No.

I swing my gaze up.

His eyes search mine, and he frowns.

"What are you doing here?" I croak.

"I've messed up so bad. I love you, Pippa. I owe you such a big apology."

Tears prick my eyes. "I don't know if that's enough."

"No, it's not. I'll do whatever it takes for your forgiveness. I'm such a fool."

I sniff as the hot tears spill down my cheeks. "You humiliated me. You left. You ... is it cheating if you screw around after jilting the woman you c-c-claim to love?"

He shakes his head and wraps his hand around mine. "There was no one else. I know it looked bad, but I swear—it's only been you since you came back into my life. Please, let me explain."

My head pounds, and I push myself to my feet, pulling my hand from his. "I can't do this."

He nods slowly. "Okay, but I'm not going anywhere."

"What's the point?"

Deacon drops his arm. "The point is that I love you and I hurt you. You never deserved it. I'm fighting for *us*, Pippa."

"There is no us."

I storm off in the direction of my house with heavy footsteps falling behind me. When I reach the base of the steps, a gentle tug on my arm has me turning back toward him.

"I don't expect you to forgive me today, but I do want you to know how sorry I am. My mum ..." He closes his eyes and huffs out a breath. "I thought you'd betrayed me—betrayed my trust. And I was so wrong, baby. Everything's been so wrong since *that* day, and you're the only thing that makes any sense. I let her cloud my judgment and hurt you in the process."

For a moment, I just stare at him. I've got no idea what happened, but the pain radiates off him in waves.

"Please send my regards to Adeline." I wrench my arm from his grasp and run the rest of the way back to the house before slamming the door shut behind me.

Falling to the floor, I sob.

Chapter Thirty-Three

Deacon

The tears in Pippa's eyes are like death by a thousand paper cuts.

I know they're not the first she's shed over me, and even though I never want to make her cry again, I doubt they'll be the last while we work through this.

Adeline?

Anger burns through me. I told her what would happen if she hurt Pippa. How the hell do I make Pippa believe nothing happened?

I pull out my phone and stalk back toward my rental house. Dialling Garrett, I fume while the other end rings out.

"Hi, this is Garrett. I'm sorry I can't take your call ..."

"Hey, it's me. I need your help. Call me back."

I pace the expansive living room while I wait. Pippa looked how I feel. She's lost weight, enough that those curves of hers that I love have started to fade.

I'm guilty of doing that to her.

That haunted look in her eyes is all my fault.

Anger ripples through me. It wasn't enough that I broke my girl's heart—I trampled on it. And unbeknownst to me, Adeline of all people helped.

Now to deliver on my promise.

By the time my phone buzzes, I am full of rage.

"What?" I snap without looking to see who it is.

"Hey. You asked me to call you back."

"Garrett."

He pauses. "Are you okay?"

"No. Do you know anything about Adeline getting in touch with Pippa?"

The silence isn't welcome.

"She posted a photo on Instagram and tagged Pippa into it. I wanted to talk to you about it, but you weren't exactly in the mood for talking last time I saw you."

Holy shit. I warned her—I warned her what would happen, and now I'll move heaven and earth to do it.

"Mallory wants to kill her. Seriously. She's that angry. And I almost wish she still had a contract with us that we could cancel. What the hell were you thinking?"

For some reason, it's reassuring when Garrett reacts that way. He made his feelings clear the night he dumped Adeline as the face of Infinity Drinks, but the anger in his voice just confirms how angry he is too.

"I was in Paris having a drink when she took a selfie before I realised. I warned her not to hurt Pippa with it—I know how that woman's mind works, but she did it anyway."

He lets out an exasperated sigh. "How is Pippa?"

"Hurting. We didn't talk for long today, but she knows I'm here. I broke her, Garrett. It's up to me to work out how to put her back together again."

"I'm guessing payback is in order?"

"You could say that."

He chuckles. "Well, you'll never guess who Adeline's been buttering up to work with?"

"Who?"

"Jacob Preston."

I grin. "You're kidding."

Garrett chuckles. "I got a call from him yesterday. After we dumped her, she got in touch with him. She thought it'd make us look bad if she jumped from us to them."

Shaking my head, I puff out a breath. "We might be in similar markets, but it's not really comparable."

"She clearly thinks it is. Anyway, Jacob was considering it because of her profile, and I told him what I thought without telling him about Pippa. But if you call him ..."

"I can cut her off at the knees." I play with my bottom lip between my teeth. "He met Pippa. They got on quite well."

Garrett hums in agreement. "Give him a call."

"Thanks, Garrett."

"No problem. And Deacon?"

"Yes?"

"For what it's worth, I hope you get your girl back. I don't know what happened, but you two were great together. She's good for you."

"Thanks."

I blow out a long sigh when the call disconnects. I've got a long road ahead of me—one that might just end in not getting Pippa back.

But I have to try.

I pull up Jacob's contact on my phone and dial. He answers almost immediately.

"Hey, Jacob. It's Deacon Miller."

"Deacon? Holy shit." He lets out a nervous laugh. "I'm surprised to hear from you. Is everything okay?"

I open my mouth before closing it again. Of course he doesn't know the story behind me leaving, but he will know I left Pippa behind.

"Not really, but I plan on making everything right. And I need your help."

"Anything. Just name it."

I suck in a sharp breath. "Have you offered Adeline Walsh a contract?"

He pauses. "Not yet. We're still talking. Do you have an objection to me working with her?"

"She hurt Pippa." I close my eyes. "I mean, I know I hurt Pippa, but I'm doing what I can to make amends and get her back. But Adeline purposefully sent Pippa a photo that she knew would hurt her while Pippa was already down over what I did ... Hell, I'm not explaining this well."

"I get the gist. What was this photo?"

"Nothing terrible. I was messed up, ran off to Europe, and ended up in a nightclub. Adeline found me. She sat next to me. She took a selfie of us together before I even realised it was her. I told her to fuck off, and what would happen if she used that photo to hurt Pippa ..."

He sighs. "Nasty. I've been told she's a bit of a diva, but I thought that wouldn't matter. She's been a part of some really successful campaigns for you. But I won't sign her if she's okay with hurting Pippa."

I let out a sigh of relief.

"I'm not doing this as a favour to you, Deacon. I like Pippa. She deserves better than what you did to her too."

Scrubbing my face with my free hand, I nod to myself. "I know. I'll be doing everything I can to make it up to her."

"That's a pretty big ask."

"I'll tell you the whole story some time."

He snorts. "You do that. In the meantime, give Pippa my regards. Garrett told me she quit. But if she ever wants a job, there's one for her with me."

"Over my dead body," I growl.

Jacob chuckles. "That's more like the Deacon I know and love."

"Thanks, Jacob."

"No problem. Now, go get your girl."

When I end the call, I smile to myself. Adeline won't know what hit her. I don't care what it takes.

And this is just the start.

There's one more call to make—one to the lady herself. I want her to know I'm behind this. I want her to know I'm happy to inflict pain on her for hurting my girl.

My phone buzzes with an incoming text. *Garrett.* A smile crosses my lips when Adeline's contact pops up.

She's going to wish she never crossed me.

After dialling her number, I tap my finger on my thigh as I wait for her to answer.

"Adeline Walsh." She answers the phone so bright and breezy, and I smirk thinking about the message I'm about to deliver.

"Adeline, it's Deacon Miller."

"Deacon, it's so good to hear from you," she practically purrs down the phone.

Is she for real? "Really? I thought given our last conversation you wouldn't be so happy to hear from me."

There's silence for a moment. "Deacon, I ..."

"I told you that if you hurt Pippa with that photo, you were done."

She pauses again. "I didn't ... I mean, you were out partying and I thought—"

"You sent it to her?"

Adeline laughs, and it's like a red rag to a bull.

"I realised you can't hurt my career. I've already been dumped by your company. What's the worst you can do?"

I smirk. She's about to lose the plot.

"Well, for starters, you won't be doing any advertising for Jacob Preston."

She gasps. "You can't—"

"I already did. Jacob likes Pippa. And he doesn't like anyone who deliberately hurts her. Am I continuing down this path, Adeline? Should I be digging into who else might be interested in employing you?"

"I'm sorry," she whispers.

"I'm not the one you should be apologising to. If you don't apologise to Pippa, then I'll just keep on going."

"I ... I ... I'll call her."

"See that you do. Goodbye, Adeline." I disconnect the call and throw my mobile on the table.

To win Pippa back, I have to show her how important she is to me. No matter how long it takes, I'll do the hard work to prove that to her.

There's a long road ahead of me, but she's worth it.

Chapter Thirty-Four

Pippa

Any aspirations for a better night sleep were dashed by around 3 a.m. this morning.

Tossing and turning all night was already my thing, but Deacon's arrival has made it even worse. Plus, there's the churning in my stomach every time I picture his sad eyes.

He seems sincere, but my reluctance to trust him again might just be the undoing of any hope I had for us.

When I do fall asleep, my dreams are weird. Deacon's running away with Adeline Walsh, and I'm running after them, but I can never catch up.

Tap tap tap.

My eyes flicker open.

Tap tap tap.

Is that the door?

I'm only dressed in sleep shorts and a tank top, so I push myself up and slip my bathrobe around me.

I pull the door open and meet the blue eyes I know so well.

"Deacon? What are you doing?"

He flashes me that panty-dropping smile that caught me the first time. "Bringing you breakfast. I know how much you like ham and cheese croissants, and you're cranky until you've had your first coffee of the morning."

Scrubbing my face with my hands, I take a moment to process that sentence. It's like nothing ever happened.

"I ... why are you here? Did you stay here last night?"

He turns and points at the house next door. Compared to my parents' place, the Larsen house is huge. It's at least five bedrooms with a verandah running all the way around. I spent a large part of my childhood wishing that was our beach house.

"I'm staying right next door. And I'm here for the duration."

My brows twitch. "Duration?"

"As long as it takes, Pip. I'm not going anywhere. I want to be right here to show you how sorry I am and try and find a way forward with you." His jaw clenches. "I didn't know Adeline sent you that picture."

I blink rapidly. "Well, she did."

"Nothing happened." He shoves his hands in his pockets. "I went out to a club for a drink, and she showed up. She sat beside me and took the photo before I realised what was really happening. I turned her down. She said some shit. I made it clear that I didn't want her. I made it clear I only wanted you."

My throat tightens.

"And then I told her if she used that selfie to hurt you, I'd destroy her career."

I lick my suddenly dry lips. "You did?"

"And yesterday I made a phone call that messed up the deal she wanted. I'll keep doing that forever to make her pay for what she did to you."

My heart thuds. Why the sudden turnaround? He hated me enough to walk away on what was the biggest day of my life. Why am I even listening to him?

Because I want to know why.

"Why did you leave me?" I croak.

He hesitates, just for a moment. "Can I come in?"

I shake my head. "No. Just tell me."

All my feelings of inadequacy come flooding to the surface. Was I just not enough for him? Is this where he tells me our relationship was a mistake? Why is he here?

Part of me wishes he'd left well enough alone because I'm not sure I'll like the answer.

"Mum came to see me the night before the wedding."

"What?" My head's in a spin. Deacon made it clear to her that he didn't want her there—I know he did.

"She made me believe—no, that's not right. She got in my head and told me she was still seeing Lucas."

I gasp. "That's a lie."

"I know that now." He winces. "But there are things I didn't tell you about Mum and Dad's split and how much it fucked me up. She ... she had photos of you and Lucas at lunch with her."

For a moment, I study him. His expression crumples, and my chest tightens at the sight.

"She told me you knew all about her still being with Lucas. I felt betrayed."

"You believed her?" Tears well in my eyes.

"Yes. I'm an idiot. I shouldn't have, but I'm so messed up, Pippa. What I should have done was come and see you, talk to you, have you wrap your arms around me and reassure me that I was wrong. Instead, I fucked up everything."

I drop my gaze. It's all a lot to take in. Deacon didn't trust me—instead he trusted a woman who did nothing but lie to him.

"There's more I need to tell you, but ..." He sighs. "It's all a lot to deal with."

He reaches out and runs his thumb down my cheek, swiping away a tear.

"I thought I wasn't good enough."

Deacon shakes his head. "Are you kidding? I'm the one who isn't good enough for you. At the very first test, I ran. I'm here because I want to put things right because I destroyed the one good thing in my life, and I'm so in love with you." He drops his hand and takes a step back. "Go and have breakfast. I'll see you tomorrow morning."

I'm left standing in the doorway—coffee in one hand, a warm paper bag in the other, wondering how on earth my life changed again in the space of twenty-four hours. It was only yesterday that I sat on the beach, my mind in turmoil over how I could start over.

Now my past is right in front of my face and I'm not sure how long he'll persist, but I have no intention of leaving. This is *my* recovery place that he's invaded.

Wrapping my head around everything he's told me won't be easy. His mother's a monster. I knew that. Maybe there's more to learn about what happened after he left town, but I'm not that surprised she messed with him.

After all, she had the balls to come after me that day.

There's a paper napkin tucked inside the bag with the croissant, and I pull it out and place it on the coffee table when blue ink catches my eye.

Curious, I pick up the napkin and unfold it.

I love you.

Where was this man on my wedding day?

———

It's late afternoon when my phone starts buzzing.

Unknown number.

Nine times out of ten, I ignore those, but there's always the odd time I get curious and answer. And being out here without a lot of human contact, that's happening more and more often. "Hello?"

"Pippa? It's Adeline Walsh."

My teeth grind so hard, my jaw aches. "What do you want?"

She takes in a sharp breath. "I deserve that."

"I'm sure this isn't a social call, so just get it over with."

Is this the part where she rubs in that she was with Deacon? He says nothing happened, but I'm not sure if I can trust him after he didn't trust me.

"I'm sorry I tagged you in that photo. I saw him and I took the picture before he even realised it was me. Nothing happened. He told me to get lost."

I swallow hard. "Why are you telling me this?"

"Because he told me he'd destroy my career if I hurt you. I just lost a potential job because of it."

"So, you're calling me because you lost a job—not because you're sorry."

"Wait ..." She sighs. "I guess, but I really am sorry. I've worked for Infinity for ages, and I thought I knew Deacon, but I didn't. He was so angry with me and he did warn me what would happen, but I thought ..."

"You thought that if he left me, he wouldn't care about what happened after."

There's silence for a moment.

"Yes. I'm sorry."

"Thank you for letting me know." I kill the call because talking to her any more is just a big waste of my time.

She really did lose a job because of that photo.

If Adeline went to the trouble of tracking down my number to apologise, she must be terrified he'll do what he threatened.

As dusk falls, the lights flicker on next door.

I sit in my darkening living room, my gaze fixed on the other house.

I'm still in the dark as to why Deacon left me, even after he said something about his mother making him think I'd betrayed him. Why the hell would he believe his mother after her past behaviour?

No matter what happened, Deacon chose to abandon me on our wedding day and leave me to pick up the pieces.

I need to tell him about the baby.

Chewing my bottom lip, I lean back on the couch and look up at the ceiling.

No. Not yet.

If this is some masterplan by Deacon to win me back, I need to let it play out. I need to know he wants me for me and not just for the baby.

I'm so unsure about whether to trust him or not.

I want to believe he's here because he wants me, but it's hard to forget the hurt and humiliation of my wedding day.

It'd be so easy to fall into his arms again, but I have far too much pride for that after everything he put me through.

Being jilted was painful enough.

His jaunt around Europe made it hurt more.

He'll have to prove to me he means what he says.

I won't settle for anything less.

Chapter Thirty-Five

Pippa

The coffee and croissants become a daily occurrence.

Deacon never uses them as an excuse to hang around. He delivers them, tells me he loves me, and then leaves again.

He must be working from the Larsen's house next door.

The notes continue. Every day, another sentence is scribbled on the napkin—each one telling me how he's feeling.

I miss your smile.

I miss waking up with you in my arms.

I miss the sound of your laughter.

I miss kissing you.

Don't give up on me.

Have dinner with me tonight. 7.00 p.m.

By the end of the week, he's begun to chip away at the icy wall around my heart. It's clear he's going nowhere.

He's determined to wait me out.

I assume he's working remotely because the Deacon I know wouldn't take this much time off work—not after he's already been away a month.

There are so many questions to be answered. I'm not sure

whether to let him back into my life or not, but to make any kind of decision, I need to know everything.

The apology from Adeline left me unsettled. He's fighting for me—there wasn't any need for him to do what he did, but he wants back in enough to be out there dealing with the Adelines of this world.

He did tell me once he'd fight my dragons.

After a week of the breakfasts and the notes, I'm done holding him at arm's length for an explanation.

By midday, I give up and make my way across the sand.

The speed at which he opens the door after I knock is enough to give me whiplash. It's like he was poised, just waiting for me to arrive.

"Pippa? This is a nice surprise."

"Why aren't you at work? It's the middle of the day."

He shoves his hands in his pockets and shrugs. "You're more important."

"I just wanted to let you know I'll be here for dinner. I've got questions."

Deacon nods. "I'm surprised you haven't asked them earlier."

Swallowing hard, I shrug. "You being here is confusing. It's taken me time to get my head together."

He reaches for me, grasping my chin and pulling my gaze to his. "Take as long as you need, Pippa. I'm not going anywhere."

"You're infuriating."

Deacon pops a kiss on my nose and lets me go. "I'm here when you want to talk. I'll tell you everything—even the things I should have originally told you."

"What does that mean?"

"Whenever you're ready, Pippa. Come and see me." He turns to walk away before looking over his shoulder. "I won't push myself on you any further. But I am enjoying bringing you breakfast in the morning."

Despite myself, I smile. I enjoy that too.

I stop on the way back and stare out to sea for a while. Deacon's presence is unnerving, but I'd still rather be here than anywhere else right now. There are some big decisions coming in my future, and although I'm delaying making them, things will come to a head soon.

I've got to start looking for a new job, but this is the first time in my life I've just had time out, away from everything and everyone—at least until Deacon arrived.

Screw it.

I'm having dinner with him, but I think I'll go into the township for lunch. I need some groceries anyway.

It's only a few minutes away, but I jump in the car and make the short drive.

After a coffee at the cafe, I'm feeling a bit more settled and head to the local Four Square. It's not a big grocery store, but then again there aren't a lot of people out here for it to service. We're probably lucky it's here at all.

Mrs Lewis waves at me from behind the only checkout. "Hi, dear. You're still here?"

I nod. "Yep. Will be for a little while, I think."

After heading toward the first shelf, I grab a loaf of bread.

"I hear you've got a handsome new neighbour."

Resisting an eye-roll, I move to the next shelf.

"I also hear he paid a lot for that house. Gabrielle Larsen was very happy."

I come to a halt—my arm in midair as I'm reaching for the breakfast cereal.

Wait. What?

"He did what?" I drop my arm and turn back toward Mrs Lewis.

"She was in here crowing about it. The first offer was for well over the last valuation, and when they refused it, he offered even more. It was just too hard for them to turn down."

It takes me a moment to process what she's said.

"Deacon bought the house?"

She gives me a smug smile. "He's already introduced himself? Sounds like a winner to me. Maybe he can help you get over that idiot who jilted you."

I scrub my face with my right hand. "He *is* the idiot who jilted me."

Her eyes widen.

Oh. I shouldn't have said that.

By the end of the day, all the locals will know.

"He must be pretty set on winning you back then."

I shrug. "I guess."

Why would Deacon have bought the house? I assumed the Larsens had rented it to him in some kind of Airbnb situation, but buying it? The man has more money than sense.

Now I need to talk to him again. Forget waiting for dinner.

I dash through the store, grabbing what I need—hell, I'm sure I've forgotten half of it.

Mrs Lewis smiles knowingly at me as I make a mad dash out the door and run to the car. I'm not sure why I'm running. It's not like Deacon's going anywhere.

After dropping off the groceries, I race across the sand to the other house again before hammering on the door until I hear a sound inside.

"Just a minute," he calls.

The door swings open.

Oh my.

He's fresh out of the shower, a blue towel wrapped around his waist and nothing else. He always looks so good.

"Pippa? You're here." The breath he lets out is audible, like he's relieved to see me. "Two visits in one day. How did I get to be so lucky?"

"Is it true? You bought the house?"

He beams that blinding smile at me. "I did. How did you ...?"

"Mrs Lewis at the store told me. Why?"

Holding up a finger, he turns back into the house. "Just give me a minute to finish getting dressed and we'll talk."

My throat tightens as I watch him walk away.

"Come in and take a seat. I won't be a minute."

Stepping into this house for the first time, I'm not disappointed. When I was a girl, I was fascinated by this place—it's so much bigger than my parents' beach house. It's fairly bare—not decorated with family photos and mementos as our house is. I didn't see any house movers, so I guess he must have bought it fully furnished.

The living room has azure walls, and the lounge suite is a deep red—reminiscent of the colour of the gown I wore at the launch party.

I sigh as I run my hand over the back of the couch before sinking into the seat.

Moments pass before Deacon walks back out. "I didn't realise you were coming over early."

"I didn't plan on it."

He drops onto the couch beside me, and I suck in a breath. I don't have to see him standing to know his blue jeans hug those muscular thighs, and he's still buttoning his shirt. It's all kinds of distracting.

"I'm glad you're here." His warm smile sucks me in.

I know he wants me back. Every day he works a little further into my heart, but I'm still unsure.

"And yes, I bought this house."

"Why?"

He pauses before blowing out a long breath. "You were ... eight maybe? And we came here for the summer holidays."

My eyebrows shoot up. Deacon and Lucas were fifteen, and that was the summer that was all about girls. Jealousy ate at me while the sound of giggling carried through the air from different parts of the beach.

The last person he was thinking of that year was me.

"You told me how much you loved this house, and you dreamed of buying it as an adult and living out here."

"I can't believe you remembered that."

He cocks his head. "Your family was always so welcoming. I remember a lot about the time I spent with all of you. And somewhere in a box at home, I still have a picture you coloured in for me of a dragon. I think you were five."

I bark out a laugh. "No, you do not."

"I do." His eyes dance with mischief, and I'm not sure I believe him. "One day, I'll dig it out and show you."

Laughing, I shake my head. "That's insane."

Deacon places his hand on my arm. "I told you. You were always important to me." He frowns. "And I should have known better that night. I should have come to you, no matter how superstitious you were being, and talked to you face to face."

I can't say anything as the conversation takes a serious turn and my stomach falls thinking about it. "Yes. You should have."

"I'll forever regret that, Pippa. And my actions afterward. There's still a lot we need to talk about. Will you stay so we can talk?"

It's all so much to take in. He bought my dream beach house because I liked it when I was eight.

Eight.

Lucas would tease me about how annoying I was, but all I wanted to do was hang out with the older boy I had such a crush on.

Deacon never called me names, even back then. He never had a bad word to say. And it turns out he paid more attention to what was going on around him than I thought he did.

I nod. "I'll stay."

Chapter Thirty-Six

Deacon

I hurt Pippa so much.

She's lost weight and she's pale. Not even the sea air is making her cheeks glow the way they used to. It's clear she's doing the bare minimum to take care of herself.

I did this.

This is all my fault.

"After I've finished, if you want to walk away then I'll respect that. I just hope you believe me when I say I'm truly sorry for what I did, and if I could turn back the clock I'd never have left."

She blinks back tears and nods. "Okay."

"I love you, Pippa. There's no one else for me but you."

Pippa sucks on her bottom lip and drops her gaze.

"I didn't tell you the full story about what happened when Dad walked in on Lucas and Mum."

Her brows dip.

"You know we left a week later. That week was so full of nastiness, and it was so toxic. Not just between Mum and Dad."

"Oh, Deacon," she whispers.

"Mum was angry that I decided to go with Dad. We had argument after argument over it. I don't know why she thought I'd take her side, but she told me that Dad was her soulmate and I'd ruined everything by being born."

Tears well in her eyes.

"She took no responsibility, and she blamed me for bringing Lucas into our lives."

Pippa reaches for my hand. "What? You two were friends since you were in primary school."

I shrug. "She blew up our family and then refused to take any blame. I should have seen a therapist or something—both Dad and I should have. But we just moved away from the problem."

Tension eats at my stomach. "There's something else I need to tell you. Lucas doesn't know this—no one does." I give her hand a squeeze. "Dad was such a mess. He worked himself to the bone in his new job trying to forget Mum. I wanted this drinks company to take off so badly so I could help him retire—although he was so stubborn, and I'm not sure he would have. It did, but it was too late. He killed himself."

Tears roll down her cheeks, and I wipe them away with my fingers.

"She spent so many years tearing him down and telling him he wasn't enough. And then the night before our wedding ..."

She squeezes my fingers. "She showed up."

"She got into my head, and I let her. I'm so sorry, Pippa. Maybe if I'd dealt with it back then, I wouldn't have been so easy for her to get to. But I felt like that vulnerable young man whose parents' marriage had exploded all over again, and I didn't shut her down like I should have."

Pippa swipes away the tears that have rolled down her cheeks.

"I drained the minibar. And I made the worst decision of my life. I'm sorry I didn't trust you. You never gave me a reason not to."

I'm such a bastard. I should have gone to her that night and talked to her about it. Even if I had doubts, I should have spoken to Pippa and trusted her.

My lack of trust and the urge to get revenge on Lucas bubbled away in the background, and when Mum pressed the right button, I blew up my own life. Pippa was collateral damage.

"I love you, Pippa, and I never stopped no matter how things looked. It's been you since the moment you walked into my office."

Her smile is faint but it's there.

"You were never meant to be my PA."

She barks out a laugh. "What?"

"I saw your recruitment office file. And at first, I thought how much Lucas would hate it if we got together, but once you stepped foot in my office, I was a goner."

Her face falls. "You were going to use me to get back at Lucas?"

"No." I lace our fingers. "I had a brief thought before squashing it because I couldn't do that to *you*. And like the greedy man I am when it comes to you, I told Garrett he could have Simone because you were mine."

Her sapphire blue eyes study me closely. "Who was I to you?"

I curl my lips into a smile. "My Pipsqueak."

She laughs, and it's glorious. I never want to make her cry again.

"It didn't take me long to realise I wanted to spend the rest of my life with you." I raise our joined hands to my lips and kiss the back of hers. "And then I let her get into my head."

Pippa draws closer before leaning her head on my shoulder. "I hate her."

I kiss the top of her head. "Me too. Lucas told me the whole story of how they ended up together. She's a predator."

Raising her head, she meets my gaze. "What do you mean?"

"She abused your brother for years. He was just ... I don't know ... immature and flattered by the attention. But it started when he was young, and I had no idea."

Her eyes search mine. "I don't understand. How could that happen right under everyone's noses?"

I sigh. "I'm not sure, but I believe Lucas. And I'll never let that woman into our lives ever again. I told him he should speak to the authorities. It might be too late to do anything about her, but he won't know until he tries."

"You're a good man," she whispers.

"I want to be *your* man again."

Pippa buries her face in my neck. "I'm so scared."

I close my eyes, breathing in the scent of her skin and raising my hand to stroke her cheek. "I know."

"I love you so much. I don't know if I'll survive you breaking my heart again."

My chest tightens. What I did to my woman will haunt me the rest of my days. "You might not believe my promises yet, but I swear I'll never hurt you again. I'm pointless without you."

"What about all the partying you did when you were away?"

I run my hand down her spine. "Smoke and mirrors. I was miserable. All I wanted was you. I'm not interested in any woman other than you."

She raises her head. Her eyes are more blue than green today. I always loved the way they look different all the time. She's so beautiful, and I'm so close to making her mine again.

Pippa swallows hard. "And Adeline?"

"I took care of that."

"She called me and apologised."

I smirk, and Pippa's mouth falls open.

"I warned her at the time not to use that photo to hurt you. She didn't listen." I pop a kiss on her forehead. "She just missed out on what could have been a big modelling job for her with Jacob Preston."

"No." Pippa's eyes are wide.

"After we dumped her, she tried her luck. Jacob was going to offer her the work, but he wasn't happy she hurt you."

"I can't believe it."

I tuck a lock of hair behind her ear. "Believe it, Pip. I'm here for you, and I'm sorry it hasn't always been that way. I'll spend the rest of my life making up for it if you'll let me."

Pippa leans back and scrubs her face with her hand. "This is all so much. I need to think. Can I give dinner a miss and sleep on it?"

Disappointment floods my veins, but she's right. She's just had all this information dumped on her, and I'm still reluctant to push her too hard. "Of course. How about we have that dinner tomorrow. And you can ask me anything."

She smiles, and for the first time since I've been here, the smile reaches her eyes. This afternoon was a big move in the right direction—not as far as I would like, but we made progress and that's what matters.

"I'll walk you home." I stand and offer her my hand.

"I'm right next door."

I nod. "I know, but it's my job to make sure you get home safe."

She hesitates for a moment before taking my offered hand and standing. For a beat, I gaze into her eyes, soaking in the sight of her.

I'm such an idiot.

"I love you, Pippa."

Her gaze drops, as does my stomach.

"Let's go." I continue, ignoring that she's said nothing.

As we make our way across the sand, still hand in hand, my heart thuds. I want this walk to last forever.

The thought of saying goodbye to her hangs heavy over me.

We reach the door of her house all too soon, and she turns, finally speaking. "It's not that I don't love you ..."

I nod. "I know. I'm here whenever you're ready."

Tucking a lock of hair behind her ear, I press a long kiss to her forehead. "I just want you to know, Pip, from the day you walked into my office, it was you. It'll only ever *be* you."

As I pull away, she meets my gaze—tears in her eyes—and nods.

My heart swells with all the love I have for her. I'd like nothing more than to throw her over my shoulder and carry her into the bedroom.

But I need to wait and be patient.

And hope to hell she forgives me.

Chapter Thirty-Seven

Pippa

Can I trust Deacon not to hurt me again?

He seems sincere, but then I fell for him the first time and where did that get me?

But he's also determined, and he's not just going to go away.

Thoughts keep circulating through my mind about Lucas too. When it all blew up, Lucas stuck to his story about being in love with Elise, but it always seemed weird.

My parents came down hard on him, even though he was nineteen and they couldn't stop him from seeing her. But after that, it just stopped.

Was she worried about being caught?

It's so confusing.

And I'm so angry at her for the guilt and pain she's caused Deacon. She was at fault—no one else. But to dump all that on her teenage son?

I didn't think it was possible to hate her even more than I already did.

After picking up my phone, I dial Lucas.

"Pip. How's it going?" He sounds so happy, and I bite my bottom lip knowing that what I'm about to ask him will kill that mood.

"I'm okay."

"Deacon making a pain in the arse of himself?"

Why? Why does he still sound happy?

My brother has been my biggest cheerleader lately, but he doesn't sound remotely bothered that the man who broke my heart is trying to work his way back into my life.

"Not really. But he told me something today, and I need to talk to you about it."

"Ahhhh." His tone drops. "What did he tell you?"

"That his mother abused you. Why didn't you say anything?"

He pauses, and I hold in a breath. Everything was so messed up back then, but this is a whole other level.

"It took me a long time to admit it to myself. She groomed me. Things were going on for a long time before we were caught."

Tears well in my eyes. "Oh, Lucas. I'm so sorry."

"You weren't to know. I didn't tell anyone. The only reason I told Deacon was because you two belong together and that woman has done enough damage to all of us."

I let out a sigh. "I'm so unsure about letting him back in."

"I know you are. And whatever you decide to do, I'm behind you. Got that, little sis?"

For a moment, I close my eyes. We might have had our differences in the past, but I know my family loves me. And my brother is my biggest cheerleader. "Got it."

"Be happy, Pippa. That's all I want for you. And I'm here whenever you need me."

I swipe away the tears that have fallen down my cheeks. "I love you, Lucas."

"Love you too, my little pain in the arse."

I let out a snort. "Some things never change."

"You know, in the past I might have given you shit, but I wouldn't swap you with anyone. And I'm sorry I didn't tell you that more."

"I think I always knew. There's no one else I'd want for a brother, either."

He chuckles. "I know that's not always been true. Go get some sleep and take care of yourself. That niece or nephew of mine needs you to rest. Have you told him?"

Blowing out a breath, I snuggle the phone even closer to my ear. "Not yet. I need to know he wants me for me."

"That's fair. Call me if you need me for anything."

"I will."

"Goodnight, Pippa."

After the call ends, I head into the bedroom and strip out of my clothes. It's still early, and there are no signs of a baby bump yet, but I run my hand over my stomach.

I've got so much to think about.

———

Despite my best efforts, I have yet another sleepless night.

I have to make a decision and soon if only to get a good night's sleep.

And at the usual time, there's a knock on the door.

I don't bother rushing. He'll wait.

And I must look a sight from his raised eyebrows when I open the door.

"Are you okay?"

I shrug. "I couldn't sleep."

He holds up his offerings and smiles. "Then I'm extra glad I brought you your pick-me-up this morning."

"You're so thoughtful." I scrub my face with my hands before reaching out to take the coffee and food.

"I'll do this every morning if it makes you happy." He hands them over before leaning in to drop a kiss on my cheek.

"Why do you keep saying all the right things?"

"Come for dinner tonight, and I'll say some more."

He turns to leave, and I shove the pastry bag in the same hand as my coffee so I can grab hold of his arm. "Deacon, wait."

"What is it?"

"Don't make me wait for dinner. Come in and talk to me."

There's hope in his eyes, and it makes me smile to see it. He might have been on my doorstep every day with breakfast, but he's been patient and he's opened up to me.

He's sincere.

"Are you sure?"

"Please?"

He follows me in and when I take a seat on the couch, I pat the cushion beside me before placing the coffee cup and the paper bag on the coffee table.

"Pippa, I know I just asked, but are you sure about this? Have something to eat and a nap, and maybe ..."

I shake my head. "No. I need to say some things."

He reaches out, his hand brushing mine before he frowns and pulls back.

"Deacon. I love you. I never stopped."

His face lights up.

"But my issue is I'm not sure if I can trust you—not when you let me down so badly."

His Adam's apple bobs, and he nods. "I understand."

"So, if I let you back in, I need you to be patient. There are going to be times when I struggle with the past." Tears well in my eyes. "It's also clear to me that you're sorry and you really do want another chance."

Silence falls over us, and when I meet his gaze, he scans my expression.

"Pippa, I'll do whatever it takes. I wish more than anything that I could go back to that night before the wedding and not let her get in my head."

"I know," I whisper. "I wish I could go back in time to stop your mother from hurting Lucas."

He nods. "That too. It's all been so raw for so long, and now there's so much more to it."

"She messed both of you up."

"So, what does this mean for us?"

"I want to try again."

An uncertain expression sweeps his face. It's like he wants to grin but doesn't want to show how excited he is. But it's bursting through as his lips twitch until he can't fight it anymore and his grin is blinding. "Really?"

"This is it though. You can't break my heart again."

"Never."

He drops from the couch to his knees in front of me.

"Marry me."

"Deacon ..."

"I fucked up so badly. You deserve a redo."

There's nothing but heart in his eyes. He's laying it all on the line. "I'm scared you won't turn up again."

"Then let's not wait. We'll fly to Las Vegas today and get married."

I blink rapidly, trying desperately to process his words.

He pushes himself up and back onto the couch beside me. "Pippa. I love you. I am not about to let you go a second time. If you still want a big wedding, we'll have one, but I'd gladly marry you today if it proves to you that I'm not leaving again."

"Why Vegas? We could have a registry office wedding in the same amount of time."

His eyes search mine. "Because you missed out on our honeymoon and we were flying back through the states, so all our paperwork is in order. And because I want to do something crazy."

My lower lip wobbles. I can't help it. "My wedding dress isn't here."

What am I saying? Surely, I have bigger concerns than that.

"We'll buy a new one when we get there. And then we'll come

home and plan something public for family and friends. Trust me?"
He holds out his hand.

I swallow hard. Either I take a leap of faith here or walk away. I can't be tormented by this any longer.

"I won't let you down again, Pippa. Ever. It's you and me."

I blink back tears before sliding my hand into his. His sigh of relief warms my heart.

"There ... there's something I need to tell you first."

His brows knit in concern.

"I'm pregnant."

His expression blanks before his eyes light up, matching the grin that forms dimples at the sides of his mouth.

"You're happy? I thought you might think this was bad timing."

Deacon gives my hand a squeeze "Baby, I want *everything* with you. We lost too much time together because I trusted the wrong person. I'm not about to hold back."

He gathers me into his arms. "Let me make a call and we'll get out of here."

Deacon presses a kiss to my lips before releasing me and standing.

"We're really doing this?"

His grin lights up his entire face. "I'm not wasting another minute of my life without you. Pack a bag. We're going to Vegas."

Chapter Thirty-Eight

Deacon

I can't believe she's here. And she's carrying my baby.

When I launched my campaign to win Pippa back, I was in it for the long haul. My life makes no sense without her.

She thought I was joking when I told her we were flying to Vegas on the company jet. By the time we drove back to Auckland, it was waiting at the airport, fuelled up and ready to go.

There's a part of me that wants to herd her onto the plane to make sure she doesn't run—I know we still have a lot of trust to rebuild.

I wouldn't blame her if she did.

When we do reach the plane, I follow her on. My heart sinks when she gasps—and it sinks in she's never travelled like this before. She missed out while I stole our honeymoon.

God, I have so much to make up for.

The hostess hovers, but I make sure Pippa's all buckled into her seat—safe and with me. I almost feel like I can't take my eyes off her for a second in case this is all a dream and she disappears.

She stretches out her long legs and yawns. I lean back and gaze at my beautiful girl.

For the first time in weeks, my heart's at peace.

I'll always regret what happened, but now we can look forward and have the future together we always wanted.

"Sleep if you need to, sweetheart," I say. "There's a bed you can lie down on to rest once we're up in the air."

"I didn't have the best night last night." Her tiredness is obvious from her soft voice. "Between thinking about us and Lucas, it's enough to make anyone tired."

Sliding my hand into hers, I lean over and kiss her softly. "I've booked a suite at the Bellagio. Tonight we rest and then tomorrow we'll organise our marriage license. Then you'll be all mine."

"I've been yours for most of my life."

I squeeze her hand. "And I'll be yours for the rest of our lives."

I'll make sure she never has cause to regret this decision.

Once we're in the air, I look over at her again. Her head is back on the headrest of the seat and her eyes are heavy. "Let's go and lie down, Pip."

She smiles at me. "Sure."

After unbuckling her belt, she rises from her seat, and I lead her toward the back of the plane. As I push open the door, she gasps behind me at the sight of the queen-size bed.

"That's huge. I thought it'd be a bunk or something."

I take her hand in mine. "Nothing but the best for my girl."

"You know you don't have to join me. I'm just going to sleep."

Pulling her into an embrace, I give her a gentle kiss. "I haven't held you in my arms for weeks. I'll sleep with you."

Her expression softens. "I'd like that."

I reach for her to help her get out of her clothing, but she gently pushes me away. "You do that and neither of us will get any sleep." She laughs, and it's music to my ears.

How did I ever walk away from her?

I'll be asking myself that question for the rest of my life.

"When we get back, I'm finding a therapist," I blurt out."

She pauses, her hands on the waistline of her skirt. "You are?"

"The way I handled everything and finding out that Mum groomed Lucas—I need help."

Tears well in her eyes, and she nods. "I think that's a good idea."

"I want to be a better man for you." I flick a glance to her stomach. "And our baby. I don't want a marriage like my parents—always at each other's throats. I should have told you this a long time ago."

She cups my cheeks. "We won't be like them. They were toxic for each other. You and I—we're different."

"I'm scared I'll mess up again."

Pippa slips her arms around my neck. "Nothing's ever perfect. I'll come with you to therapy if you want me to. We do this together."

I rub her arms. "You'd do that?"

"I love you. I've loved you my whole life. As long as we keep communicating, we can get through anything together."

My throat tightens. This is one of the many reasons I love this woman so much. She's not blind to my faults, and she's willing to support me through it. I know she's not like my mother, who blames everything on everyone else and never takes responsibility.

I'm so in love with Pippa, it hurts.

"Let's catch up on some sleep before we get married." Pippa's eyes dance with excitement. "We'll deal with the real-life stuff when we get back."

With a tender kiss, she drops her arms and then pushes her skirt to the floor. I've missed her so much. She climbs into the bed, pulling the covers over her, and I slide in beside her.

I caress her soft skin and run my hand over her stomach where the smallest of baby bumps has begun.

"I can't believe we're having a baby."

"Better get used to the idea. We've got seven months to get ready."

I laugh against the back of her neck and breathe her in.

"I wish I'd been there when you found out. There's no way I want to miss another second of this pregnancy."

She lets out a soft sigh. "You're here now. That's all that matters."

And together, against the hum of the plane engines, we drift off to sleep.

Chapter Thirty-Nine

Pippa

By the time we reach our destination, I'm relaxed and well rested.

I didn't realise just how much I missed Deacon's warmth in bed while I slept until I woke up with him curled around me.

Despite Deacon being by my side, I'm still nervous about whether we'll make it to the altar.

He hasn't put a step wrong, but my heart has been trampled so hard that I'm not sure I could take any more.

It's so difficult to let him out of my sight.

Together we go to apply for a marriage licence—he even comes with me to find a dress. I think he's as scared to lose sight of me as I am of him.

When we're back in our hotel room, he gets online to find a wedding chapel.

I know he's found what he's looking for when he whoops and punches the air. I move to sit beside him to take a look, and he holds out a palm.

"Wait one second. I want to book this because it's perfect, and then we'll talk."

My eyes narrow. "What are you hiding from me?"

"Nothing." He beams an innocent smile at me, but it doesn't quell my suspicions. "But I can book this for this evening, and then I just have to pop downstairs to do some shopping before we leave to get married."

"This is insane, you know."

His grin is infectious. "I know, but you're going to love it. I promise."

I sit in a chair nearby and cross my arms, watching him as he focuses on the screen. I'm sure I could sneak over and peek, but he's so excited, I don't want to ruin his buzz.

When he's finished, he closes the laptop and gets up. He walks toward me and leans over, planting a kiss on my lips.

"Is there anything you need while I'm out?"

I nod. "Can you bring back food?"

"Call room service. The menu's by the phone. I won't be too long."

"What are you up to, Deacon Miller?"

He grins again. "Just making today memorable. By the way, the chapel will do both video and photos, so we can share all of this with the family."

I grimace. "Mum's going to kill me."

Deacon shrugs. "Maybe, but you'll at least be a beautiful bride today."

Reaching behind me, I pull a cushion out from behind my back and smack his arm with it. "That doesn't help."

With a laugh, he turns and heads toward the door. "Love you, Pip."

"Love you too, jerk face."

He's still laughing as he leaves, and despite my irritation that he's keeping secrets, I can't help but smile.

———

By the evening, I'm champing at the bit to know what's going on.

Deacon continues to leave me in the dark while cajoling me with food—it's a winning strategy.

"It's time to get dressed. There's a car picking us up in around half an hour."

I glare at him. "What else?"

He claps his hand together. "There's something you should know before we go. It's an Elvis chapel."

My mouth falls open. "No way."

"It was the earliest wedding service I could find." His eyes twinkle with mischief.

"Bullshit." I laugh. "But I love it. Let's do it."

He grins. "I just want this to be as memorable as possible. We'll have another ceremony when we get home for all our friends and family."

"One you'll turn up to?"

For a moment, he falters before he realises I'm teasing and his smile reappears. "I'll be glued to your side from now on, Pippa." He leans over and gives me a soft kiss. "Go and get dressed, and let's get married."

Once I'm ready, I walk out of the bedroom. Deacon's fiddling with his bow tie. We'll look a sight in that Elvis wedding chapel with his tux and my formal gown, but I can't wait to be Mrs Miller and draw a close to the bad in our lives.

He looks up at me and smiles. "You look beautiful. Come here."

I walk toward him, and he bends and picks up a box from the couch.

"Turn around."

His warm hand brushes my collarbone, and the cool metal of a necklace being draped around my neck touches my skin.

"What did you do?" I ask.

"Bought you something for a wedding gift. I figured it was the least I can do."

And just like the last time we were together like this, he places a kiss on my shoulder.

I close my eyes.

"I love you, Pippa. You're the best thing that ever happened to me."

When I turn back to him, he smiles.

I look down at the necklace. It's similar to the ruby pendant he bought me, but this time it's sapphire. The shade of blue reminds me of his eyes.

"Lord knows I'm not perfect, but it's new and blue."

He leans over and places a gentle kiss on my lips.

"It's wonderful. I love it."

Reaching for my hand, he knits our fingers together and squeezes.

A limo's waiting for us outside the hotel, and we're swept away down the strip to the chapel.

"Nervous?" Deacon asks.

I nod. "A little."

"It'll just be us, the celebrant, and a witness. And then once the ceremony is over, you're all mine."

He leans close to me, and I rest my head on his shoulder.

Am I doing the right thing?

I guess time will tell, but it feels right.

"This is kinda crazy, Deacon. What are we doing?"

He chuckles. "I'm setting things right. And yeah, it's crazy. I know we could have gotten married back home, but this is more exciting, right?"

I raise my head. "That's one word for it."

"I'm giving you a wedding to remember, and then we can head home for a while before we take a honeymoon."

I turn my head. "You just took a month off work."

He shrugs. "They'll survive. You can pick where we go. If you want to go to Europe, we can do that. If you want somewhere closer to home ..."

"Do you want my honest opinion?"

He nods. "It's your choice, so sure."

"I want to go home to our new beach house."

Deacon grins and leans over, kissing me. "We'll do that then. And then on our first anniversary, we'll take a trip."

"I love that idea." I cup his cheek. "And I love you."

"I'll never get sick of hearing that."

The limo pulls to a stop, and the driver opens the door before offering me his hand as I step out onto the kerb. Deacon follows me, slipping his arm around my waist and leading me toward the chapel.

It's dream-worthy.

In the heat and the dust of the Nevada desert is this tiny church-looking building. There's a colourful garden around it, and as Deacon leads me along the path to the front door, I let out a sigh.

"This is amazing."

"As soon as I saw it, I knew we had to be married here. It's so you."

"You know me so well."

When we reach the steps, the Elvis celebrant and a woman are waiting for us.

"Welcome, little lady," he says, and I giggle. "Let's get you two hitched."

Deacon gives my waist a squeeze and we follow them into the chapel.

It's just as pretty on the inside. Candlelight makes the wooden walls glow warm and welcoming, and once Deacon sorts out the paperwork, our ceremony starts.

I spend my time switching my gaze between Elvis and Deacon. The ceremony won't be long—we've got the chapel booked for half an hour and that includes two songs from Elvis.

This is insane. I can't believe this is my life.

And I love every single second.

When it comes to the rings, I panic for a microsecond before Deacon draws two boxes out of his pocket.

"I got it covered, Pipsqueak. I've got your engagement ring too. It's time to put it back on."

Inside the boxes are new white-gold rings. He's thought of everything.

I'm teary-eyed as we exchange them.

"Now it's time for the vows. Deacon, what do you have to say to your little lady?"

Deacon turns to me and takes my hands in his. He draws in a deep breath. "I messed up. And when I did, I hurt the person I love more than life itself. So, this is me, Pippa, promising to make all your dreams come true and never, ever hurt you again. I swear I'll never make you cry, and I'll slay all your dragons. From today until the end of time, I'll be there for you."

Tears well in my eyes. Deacon's sincerity is blinding even in comparison to the bright lights of Vegas. If I still had any doubts about how he felt, they just evaporated.

"I ... just give me a second."

"Take your time, darlin'," Elvis says.

This whole thing is so absurd, I can't help but giggle.

"Pippa?" Deacon's brows knit.

"I'm a little overwhelmed, but I'm okay."

I press my lips together briefly before blowing out a long breath and giving Deacon a nod.

"Deacon. I love you. I have loved you for as long as I can remember. There might be bumps in the road ahead, but as long as I'm with you, I know I'll be okay."

That's all I can get out before I choke up again. But I smile through the tears as Deacon squeezes my hands.

"By the power vested in me by the state of Nevada, I pronounce you man and wife. You may kiss your bride."

I grin, and Deacon dips me, pressing his lips to mine before devouring my mouth in a kiss so hot I'm about to melt into the floor.

"No getting away now."

I squeeze his hand as Elvis starts singing "Love Me Tender". He turns to me, his brow furrowed. "Pippa, I won't ever—"
"I know."

Chapter Forty

Pippa

"Let me go in first?"

Deacon and I sit in the car in the backyard of Mum and Dad's place. They'll have heard the car and know they've got visitors. But I'm not sure how they'll react to Deacon's presence.

His disappearance hurt them too.

They knew he was out at the beach—we spoke about it. But neither of them interfered or pressured me either way.

I appreciate at least being treated like an adult instead of their little girl.

Deacon nods. "I'll be right behind you, though."

Leaning over, I kiss him softly on the lips. "I know you've got my back."

"Always."

His eyes search mine. Even with the ring on my finger, I'm still struggling with trust. But he's trying, and that's important to me.

I give his forearm a squeeze and step out of the car. Taking a deep breath, I cross the yard and open the back door before stepping into the kitchen.

"Mum? Dad?"

Mum appears in the doorway leading to the living room. "Pippa? Where have you been? Your father and I have been so worried. Lucas said you weren't at the beach house and that you were safe, but he wouldn't say anything more."

I grasp Mum's forearms. "I'm here, Mum, and I'm fine. There was just something I needed to take care of."

"And you didn't think that we would want to know where you were?"

I look back over my shoulder. Deacon stands just outside, staring at his feet.

He looks up and meets my gaze. I nod.

Closing the door behind us, we make our way into the living room. Mum's moved to stand beside Dad.

"Deacon?" My dad's face is thunder as he glares at my husband.

Husband.

What a weird word.

I hold out my palm. "Dad. It's okay. Deacon and I have sorted everything out."

He frowns. "He broke you, baby girl."

Nodding, I walk toward him. "I know. But he's also putting me back together."

Deacon's hand runs down my spine until it rests on my lower back, and I don't have to turn to see how close he is.

"Are you sure?"

I lick my lips, my mouth suddenly dry. "There's something we need to tell you. Two things, actually. I'm going to need you and Mum to take a seat."

Dad glances at Mum.

I lead Deacon to the couch, and we sit as Mum and Dad lower themselves into their chairs.

Deacon gives me a reassuring smile and a wink before I start speaking.

"Deacon and I have been working on things for a little while. In fact, he's bought the house next to ours out at the beach."

My dad's eyebrows rise.

"Anyway, we got to the bottom of everything, and I was worried that he might do another runner. So ... um ..." I hold out my hand with my rings. "We flew to Vegas and got married."

Silence greets us, and Mum and Dad exchange a longer look.

"Vegas?" Dad asks.

"I didn't want to give her a chance to get cold feet on me, sir," Deacon says.

Dad huffs. "Like you did?"

"There's more to that story, Dad, and we'll tell you everything. But I just need you to let me share our other news first."

He leans back in his chair, crossing his arms. "Go on."

"I'm pregnant. Deacon and I are having a baby."

"Oh, love," Mum says softly. "That's wonderful."

"That why you married her?" Dad asks.

Deacon shakes his head. "No. I love Pippa more than anything, and I always did." He takes my hand in his and squeezes. "I know I messed up, and I hurt Pippa when that's the last thing I ever wanted. But—"

"Can't wait to hear this," Dad says.

"Dad. When we were here at Christmas, I went out shopping with Lucas and we stopped at a cafe for lunch. Deacon's mother showed up."

Dad draws in a deep breath. Like everyone else in our family, he hates Elise. And if Lucas has only confided in Deacon, then he doesn't even know the full history behind what happened.

"She started talking about my relationship with Deacon and I told her where to go. I didn't think much of it at the time, but she had someone with her—a man maybe about my age. He must have taken photos because the night before the wedding, she turned up to see Deacon and showed him a photo of us at lunch. She told him that she was still seeing Lucas and that we were all friends."

"What?" Mum gasps. "Lucas told us he hasn't—"

I shake my head. "He's not, Mum. The day they got caught by

Deacon and his dad was the last time. She's so bitter over the way Deacon turned his back on her, she wanted to hurt him. At least, that's what we think."

Deacon gives my hand another squeeze. "All these years and I'm still messed up by it. The whole thing destroyed my dad's life. I shouldn't have let her get to me, and I should have stopped to talk it out with Pippa, but after Mum left I was a mess. There's no excuse for what I did, and I will have regrets for the rest of my life over how I handled it."

Dad uncrosses his arms and leans forward. "You love her?"

"With everything I have." Deacon slides his arm around me and tugs me closer. "I'll do my best to never hurt her again. I promise you that. I'll be a good husband, and a father."

I smell Mum's familiar floral perfume before she sits on the couch beside me and grasps my forearm. "I think we should be supportive, Dale. We're going to be grandparents."

Dad huffs but slowly nods. "Are you happy, Pippa? That's what matters to us."

"I am."

Mum wraps her arms around my neck and kisses my cheek. "You know I might never forgive you for sneaking off to get married."

Tears well in my eyes and I laugh. "We'll plan another ceremony now we're home. We just wanted to make it official as quickly as possible."

"But Las Vegas?" she asks, letting go.

"That was my idea." Deacon grins. "We were going to spend a couple of days there on the way back from our honeymoon, and I wanted to try and make up for Pippa missing the Europe trip."

My gaze meets his, and he wipes the tears that have fallen onto my cheeks.

"Which we'll take together at another time, so Pippa can visit all those places she wanted to."

Dad's still a little grouchy, but Mum seems to have bounced back. "I'll make some coffee and you can tell us all about the wedding."

After reaching into my bag, I pull out a pouch of photos and hand them to Dad. "I've got these."

He takes them, his expression softening as he takes out the first one. "You look so beautiful."

"I'm sorry if you feel excluded, Dad. After everything that's happened, we wanted something for ourselves."

"I'll cover any costs for the last wedding and our new ceremony," Deacon says. "It's the least I can do."

A glimmer of a smile appears on Dad's face, and I clamp my lips together to stop myself from laughing.

"He'll be okay, love," Mum says from the doorway. "Now you're talking his language."

I take Deacon's hand in mine.

Everything will be fine.

Epilogue

Deacon

A lusty wail hurts my eardrums as I tip the bottle on my wrist to check the temperature.

Pippa's out Christmas shopping, and our daughter's decided she doesn't want to wait for Mummy to eat.

Oh thank God it's warm enough.

I gather my girl in my arms and swipe away her angry tears before lifting the bottle to her lips. Her whole demeanour changes as she kicks her legs, sucking at the teat before I've even managed to get it in position.

"You're so much like me, little bug. No patience." I laugh softly. "If you could just wait a little longer, Mummy will be back and you much prefer her to the bottle, right?"

Willow's two months old now, and at that stage where her personality is starting to shine through. Pippa didn't quite make it to full-term, but it was late enough that Willow was fine. It's not been an easy two months—she's not the best sleeper, but we take turns in the night and Pippa's been expressing milk so that I can feed her.

We've been through so much in the past few months.

I found Pippa's dream home, complete with the picket fence, and we moved in about a month before Willow arrived. And right now, she's out shopping for Christmas lunch—she insisted on us having a big family Christmas our first year in the house.

My woman's a machine, and I'm so crazy about her.

Trust was hard to come by, even after we were married, but Willow's birth brought us closer than we've ever been.

Life is good.

The rumble of the garage door makes me smile.

"Did you hear that, Willow? Mummy's home."

She doesn't care. Her eyes are closed and she's slowing down. With any luck, she'll go to sleep and I can get a few hours alone with my gorgeous wife.

There's a rustle of bags, and the internal door from the garage to the kitchen opens and closes.

"Did you get everything you needed?" I ask.

Pippa walks into the room, leans over the back of the couch, and I raise my head to let her kiss my lips.

"I did. We should have gone out to the beach and just had a barbecue."

I chuckle. "Need I remind you that it was your idea to have Christmas here this year? Next year would have been easier."

Pippa's still at home full-time with Willow right now. She never returned as my PA, but she plans on coming back when Willow turns one and I'll be more than happy to work with my wife.

"I just want our first Christmas with the whole family." She squeezes my shoulder. "I wish your dad was here."

"Me too, babe. He would have loved our girl."

"Is she asleep?"

I look back at Willow. She's pushed the teat out of her mouth and her eyes are firmly closed. "Only just. Do you need a hand getting everything out of the car?"

Pippa rounds the couch and drops down beside me. "Yes, please. Give her to me for a minute, and I'll pop her down."

Gently, I transfer my favourite little bundle into Pippa's arms and watch my girls as Pippa smiles at Willow.

"She's just had a bottle. I tried to tell her to wait a little longer for her mum, but you know how impatient she is."

Pippa laughs gently. "She takes after you in that regard."

"That's what I told her." I shrug before leaning over and pecking my wife on the lips. "I'll go sort out the car and be right back."

"Thank you. I love you." She smiles, and as like every time, it makes my heart thud. I love this woman with everything I am.

I head out to the garage, shake my head, and laugh. The car's overflowing, but I wouldn't expect anything less. Pippa wants everything to be perfect.

Her parents and Lucas arrive tomorrow, and she likes to be prepared.

Lucas and I called a permanent truce. I've been so angry with him for so many years, but after he shared his story, I saw another side that made me hurt for him.

He went to the police and also tracked down my mother's current lover, who turned out to have a similar story. It took some persuading as he was still under her spell, but he cracked when Lucas told him their history. The legal process is long with investigations ongoing, but Mum's in a lot of trouble.

I don't miss her. It took time, but Pippa's family forgave me and they're my family—not just because I'm married to Pippa. I'll miss Dad for the rest of my life, but Pippa's father has stepped in as more than a father-in-law. He's been there for me while we've worked through the past and moved on.

And Pippa?

Pippa's the best thing that ever happened to me. I'll never take her for granted after throwing away what we had once. She's patient, kind, and loves me and Willow with everything she has.

By the time I've put all the food away and brought everything in, Pippa greets me at the kitchen door.

"She asleep?"

Pippa nods. "Out like a light."

She slides her arms around my neck and gives me a tender kiss.

"Should we ... be taking advantage of this moment?"

Her face lights up. "Definitely."

"I love you." I lean forward and bury my face in her hair. "Only you, Pippa. Only ever you."

Also by Wendy Smith

Coming Home

Doctor's Orders

Baker's Dozen

Hunter's Mark

Teacher's Pet

A Very Campbell Christmas

Fall and Rise Duet

Falling

Rising

Fall and Rise - The Complete Duet

The Aeon Series

Game On

Build a Nerd

Bar None

Coming soon Love on Site

Hollywood Kiwis Series

Common Ground

Even Ground

Under Ground

Rocky Ground

Coming soon Solid Ground

Stand alones

For the Love of Chloe

Coming soon Only Ever You

The Friends Duet

Loving Rowan

Three Days

The Forever Series

Something Real

The Right One

Unexpected

Chances Series

Another Chance

Taking Chances

Lifetime Series

In a Lifetime

In an Instant

In a Heartbeat

In the End

At the Start

About the Author

Wendy Smith published as Ariadne Wayne for three years before deciding she didn't want to be someone else all the time. She's a multi platform bestselling author, whose book In the End, written as Ariadne Wayne, was named one of Apple's best books of 2017. All her stories come with a quirky sense of humour, and she cries over everything.

Find me online
www.wendysmith.co.nz
wendy@wendysmith.co.nz